SPACEPOP

ROCKING THE RESISTANCE

[Imprint]
MAKE YOUR MARK

A part of Macmillan Children's Publishing Group, a division of Macmillan
Publishing Group, LLC

SPACEPOP: ROCKING THE RESISTANCE. Copyright © 2016 by Genius Brands
International, Inc. All rights reserved.
Printed in the United States of America by LSC Communications US, LLC
(Lakeside Classic), Harrisonburg, Virginia.
For information, address Imprint, 175 Fifth Avenue, New York, N.Y. 10010.

Library of Congress Cataloging-in-Publication Data is available.

ISBN 978-1-250-10228-7 (hardcover) / ISBN 978-1-250-10229-4 (ebook)

Our books may be purchased in bulk for promotional, educational, or business
use. Please contact your local bookseller or the Macmillan Corporate
and Premium Sales Department at (800) 221-7945 ext. 5442 or by
e-mail at MacmillanSpecialMarkets@macmillan.com.

Book design by Natalie C. Sousa
Imprint logo designed by Amanda Spielman
Illustrated by Jen Bartel

First Edition—2016

1 3 5 7 9 10 8 6 4 2

mackids.com

Resist the urge to steal this book,
or you'll be taken from your reading nook;
banished and under key and lock,
cursed to never read again, sing, or rock.

SPACEP♥P

ROCKING THE RESISTANCE

ERIN DOWNING

[Imprint]
MAKE YOUR MARK
NEW YORK

SPECIAL THANKS This one goes out to all girls who stand up and fight for what's right, even when it isn't the easy thing to do

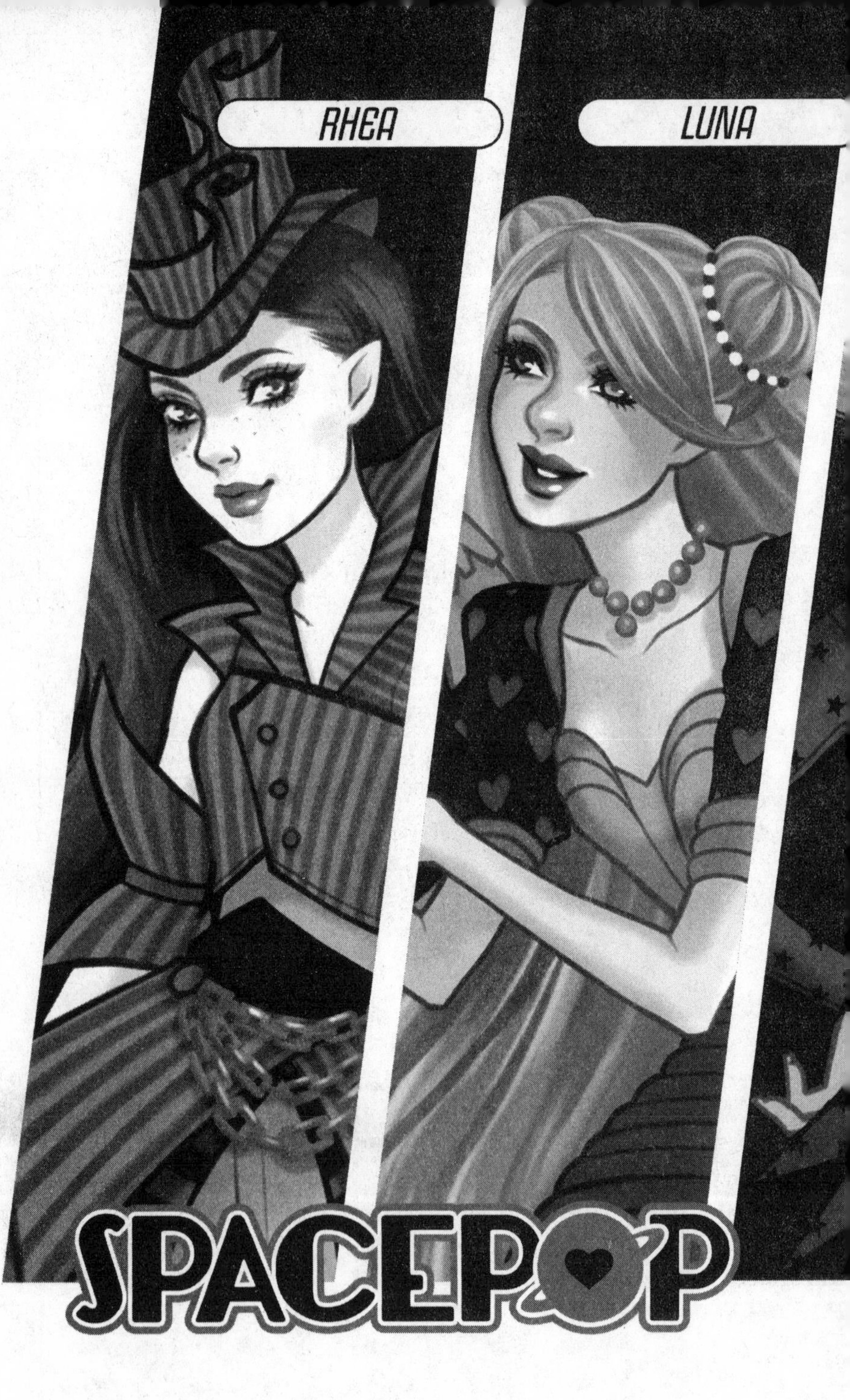
RHEA
LUNA
SPACEPOP

ATHENA

JUNO

HERA

"Greetings, all you lowly fools on the planets of the Pentangle. Guess who's back and more amazing than ever? That's right, darlings—it's me: your magnificent and all-powerful EMPRESS GEELA!

"Have you missed my beautiful face during this dark period when my media networks were on a break? I realize it may have been — ahem —an inconvenience that every single one of my news and entertainment channels was off the air for several weeks. My servers are undergoing some technical difficulties, but a team has been working hard to solve a rather sticky situation. Despite their obvious incompetence, they have finally fixed the problem so none *of you needs to suffer through life without your favorite shows any longer.*

"The Geela Entertainment Holo-Viz Networks are back—and our upcoming programming is better than ever! We'll be airing all-new, even more romantic episodes of The Empress. *Look forward to a remarkable new season of* Dancing with the Empress. *And of course, we have a full slate of incredible music programming including new songs from galactic rising stars SPACEPOP!"*

"Wait—what?! CUT!" Geela, the self-appointed Dark Empress of Evil, glared at the team of producers gathered around her elegant soundstage. She hissed, "Who is this SPACEPOP, and why must I talk about them during an announcement about *me* and *my* shows?"

Geela's newly promoted executive producer ducked his head and cringed. He was the fourth executive producer Geela had worked with that day. The first three were recovering from their morning assignments in the studio's medical wing. "Y-y-your Highness," the beefy, square-headed alien stuttered. Four slender tentacles on his head quivered.

"Speak up!" Geela snapped.

"Your Highness, SPACEPOP is that new band?" he said in a whisper. "The band that sings the song 'We 'Bout to Start Something Big'?"

"Is that a question or a statement?" Geela demanded.

The expression on her stone-cold face was impassive, her mouth set into a thin line.

"A statement, Empress." The enormous producer let out a shaky sigh. "SPACEPOP is the hottest new band in the galaxy. Athena, Rhea, Juno, Luna, Hera—"

Before he could say anything more, Geela's long, quick fingers plucked a jelly-filled doughnut off the platter floating beside her in midair. She whipped it at the producer, smirking as her sweet little missile flew across the soundstage at the speed of light. *Splurk!* Green jelly goo flew in all directions when the doughnut hit the producer's face.

"Clean that up!" Geela screamed, gesturing to the sticky mess. "And that will be *enough* talk of SPACEPOP. Let's get back to work so we can air this special message for the people of the galaxy. It's been too long since they've heard my voice. Have I made myself clear?"

Everyone in the studio mumbled, "Yes, Your Highness."

Geela nodded, scowling at her employees. Then she stood tall, smiled at the camera, and began again:

"Before we return to my exceptional slate of programming, please listen closely to an important warning. I am certain all of you are well aware that it is simply NOT POSSIBLE for anyone to break in and destroy my servers. However, if some PESKY rebels ever did manage to breach my impeccable security and steal or break something

(again), there will be consequences. I want to make sure this is crystal clear: any creature caught anywhere near MY STUFF will be captured immediately and taken to a very special storage compartment in the DUNGEON OF DARK DOOM. There, as my esteemed guest, you will learn to mind your manners and my rules.

"Now that we've gotten all this essential business out of the way, I want to take a moment to tell you all about a wonderful new product I just ADORE! The Swish-M-Boots are a marvelous invention that will absolutely REVOLUTIONIZE your cleaning routine. Take it from me—this is the greatest new product of the millennium. Is your cleaning bot on the fritz? Tired of getting down on hands and knees to reach that pesky dirt in the corners of your home? Crouch no longer! With the Swish-M-Boots, you can sway, dance, and skate your home clean. Our special cleaning pads attach to your limbs and—"

"Cut! *Cut!*" Geela screeched, waving one long arm in front of the camera. She flicked the cameraman's nose with her pointed fingernails. "This is *ridiculous!*"

The cameraman howled in pain. "I'm sorry, Your Highness. I'm so sorry. Can I get you a fresh box of doughnuts, Your Greatness? Something to cheer you up for the next take?"

"There will be no *next take*," Geela growled. "I do everything perfectly the first time."

"Of course you do," crooned the jelly-covered producer. "You're magnificent."

Geela smiled. "Indeed." Her cold smile curled into a hideous frown. "But what is this *nonsense* about Swish-M-Boots? Since when do I advertise these silly cleaning products? I am the DARK EMPRESS OF EVIL!"

All the gathered producers and other staff exchanged nervous glances. Tibbitt, Geela's beloved sidekick, hopped off the empress's shoulder and hid under a table. Finally, one of the assistant producers squeaked, "Swish-M-Boots are one of your new products, Your Highness. Your team of researchers invented them, and all the money made from sales of the boots will go directly to you. You stand to make a fortune if the product catches on."

"I see," Geela said, her nostrils flaring. "So I'm supposed to endorse this product?"

The young producer nodded eagerly. "Yes, that's correct."

"Just to be clear, you want me—the most important person in the entire galaxy—to endorse an absurd pair of boots that help clean floors?"

No one said anything.

Geela raised her arms over her head. "I have taken it upon myself to imprison the royal families of the Pentangle and rule over the galaxy, and I have proved myself to be the most influential and powerful creature alive in the universe. Yet I am supposed to smile cheerfully and tell people I CLEAN MY OWN FLOORS?" She shook her fists. "Does anyone see how utterly *nonsensical* that is?"

There was a chorus of yeses from Geela's staff.

"Whose idea was this?" Geela shouted.

Silence.

"Tell me WHOSE IDEA IT WAS TO INCLUDE THIS FOOLISH COMMERCIAL IN MY SCRIPT!" Geela slammed her fists onto a table, and her body grew rigid with fury. The room crackled with energy. Tibbitt whimpered and scooted farther under the table. As much as the empress seemed to like her strange pet, he often got caught in the cross fire when she went on one of her rampages.

"If I were selling shampoo and showing off my lustrous locks, that would make sense. As you are all aware, my hair is outstanding. Undoubtedly, my best feature." She caressed her shiny dark hair, blissfully unaware that everyone in the room knew she wore a wig. "Or if I were promoting a line of self-help books, that would also make sense since I have so much wisdom to impart. Perhaps a workout video, to help others achieve my level of physical fitness and strength." She flexed her biceps. "But CLEANING? Come on, you fools. Who's going to believe that?"

When no one said anything, Geela shook her head and hissed, "You all disgust me. Find me a new staff, then fire yourselves." She beckoned for Tibbitt to follow, grabbed another doughnut, and stormed out of the room, muttering, "I am running a galaxy full of fools . . ."

LUNA

"TAKE FORTY-SIX," A WEARY COMMERCIAL DIREC-tor called out. "And . . . action!"

"Hello, all you *gorgeous* Pentangle residents." Luna, the lead singer of the band SPACEPOP, stood with her back to the camera and shook out her long golden hair. "Love my locks? Well, let me tell you all about Solar Glow, an out-of-this-world new hair-care line that will make *your* hair look like *this!*" Luna spun around and beamed at the camera. "Bad hair days begone!"

"Cut!" someone yelled from the edge of the set. A formal-looking older fellow stepped out of the shadows, smiling apologetically. "Cut, *cut!*"

"What is it, Chamberlin?" a producer asked, obviously

irritated. One of the female alien's two heads glanced at the clock and grumbled, "We really need to wrap things up here."

The older guy—Chamberlin—stepped forward and explained, "As I've told you approximately forty-six times already, you are not to show Miss Luna's face in this commercial. We all agreed that this spot is to be only about her hair."

Luna pouted. She *loved* her hair, but her face was undoubtedly her best feature. And Luna loved for it to be seen. "But, Chamberlin—"

Chamberlin cut her off. "No buts, Your Hi—" Chamberlin stopped himself just in time. Though he had been living with the five princesses of the Pentangle for over a month, he sometimes forgot the girls were in disguise and he was no longer allowed to call any of them "Your Highness" when there were other creatures nearby. If anyone were to find out the band SPACEPOP was actually a cover for the five missing princesses, they would be in for some serious trouble. Geela and her extensive army of Android Soldiers were searching for the missing girls everywhere.

Just over a month ago, Geela had taken the kings and queens of the Pentangle prisoner and declared herself empress, and Chamberlin had been given the task of helping the princesses escape and then keeping them safe.

Though the experienced royal butler would have preferred that he and his charges hide on a remote planet until life in the galaxy was back to normal, the five princesses came up with a very different idea. Not willing to sit by quietly while their homes were destroyed, the young royals disguised themselves as a rock band called SPACEPOP and set off on a tour of the galaxy singing songs about rebellion and peace.

Eager to succeed in the most important assignment of his life—keeping the princesses safe and their true identities a secret—Chamberlin had agreed to act as the band's "manager" while they were on the road. It was not an easy job. Especially now that the band was achieving a certain level of fame for their music. Luna, especially, could be a bit of a diva. All the girls missed their royal lives.

Chamberlin cleared his throat and went on. "As we have discussed, Luna, the Solar Glow Corporation is not paying you enough to use your face in this commercial. Only hair. And no, we are not willing to negotiate." The girls' disguises were still relatively new, and Chamberlin was constantly worried about the five girls being recognized if anyone got a close-enough look at one of them. Broadcasting Luna's face in a commercial that would air all over the galaxy was too risky. When she had insisted on doing this product endorsement, Chamberlin had made her agree to certain terms.

"Got it," muttered the weary director. "No face. Only hair. But, dude, can you please inform your talent that she's as much to blame as anyone? Quit spinning around to smile at the camera, lady!"

Luna clenched her jaw. *"Excuse me?"*

The director rolled his eyes. "You heard me: quit spinning around. We can't keep your face hidden if you insist on smiling at the camera."

"Do you have any idea who I am?" Luna said. "My name is *not* 'lady.' "

"Whatever," the director muttered. "And yeah, of course I know who you are. You're this week's hot new thing. I've been in this business long enough to see plenty of singers just like you come through my studio. You and SPACEPOP are hot today, but don't get too full of yourself. It can all be gone, just like that."

Luna huffed. There were many things she disliked about living in disguise, but this was probably the worst. She hated people treating her with anything less than the full respect she deserved. She couldn't tell anyone who she really was, and there were times—like now—that she would absolutely love to announce, "I am Lunaria de Longoria, the princess of Lunaria," to see how quickly the lowly creature would bow and avert his eyes. She could just imagine the look on that sniveling director's face if he learned her true identity. *He* was full of himself for no reason. *She*, on the other hand, deserved it.

"Remember, Luna," Chamberlin whispered. "No showing your face. That was the deal we made. We can't risk you being recognized—it's for your own safety, and the safety of the other girls."

"Fine," Luna snapped. Then she sighed, thinking of how awful it would be if she ruined things for the four fellow princesses she now considered her friends—the first true friends she (or any of them) had ever really had. Quietly, she added, "I get it."

"Take forty-seven," the director grumbled. "And . . . action!"

This time, Luna swung her hair and recited her lines like a pro. She'd had plenty of experience with photo shoots during her years as princess of Lunaria, and she knew how to buckle down and get things done when she had to. Though she wasn't thrilled with the end result, she decided take forty-seven was good enough. Solar Glow was complete junk, so the commercial didn't really deserve her best effort anyway. The products smelled like chemicals, and when Luna used them in her own hair, they left her long, gorgeous waves limp and lifeless. She was pretty sure she had even detected a faint green tinge among her golden highlights. And at the edges of her face, Luna's soft buttery-yellow skin had started to burn a little after she'd left the hair mask on too long.

But because Luna liked the attention and loved that she was the only member of SPACEPOP asked to endorse the line of Solar Glow products, she had quickly said yes when she was offered the paid opportunity. The funds would help her refresh her makeup collection. Besides, she felt guilty that most of the residents of the Pentangle couldn't afford the hair creams and cleansers she used in her own hair—Solar Glow was (maybe) better than using nothing at all. Even if the things she said about Solar Glow weren't true, it's not as if a few little white lies would hurt anyone.

No one would ever have to know—just like all the other secrets she and the other princesses of the Pentangle had been keeping.

JUNO

IGNORING HER BURNING MUSCLES, JUNO SCRAM-bled onto a narrow bridge and leaped across a lava stream. The toughest and most athletic member of SPACEPOP flung her legs up and over an enormous steel column, then braced her body for impact as she jumped fifteen feet to the next level down. "Oof!"

Juno—who had once been well-known throughout the galaxy as the princess Junoia Atley-Wolford—ducked and weaved as she crossed through an open area in the warrior-style obstacle course. Small animals screeched and dove at her, pecking and burrowing into her spiky purple hair. Juno swatted them away. Thick metal branches closed in around her. Unfazed, she got down on her hands and knees and crawled, commando-style, under them. None of the obstacles thrown her way were anything compared with what she had faced when she had been sent into the wilderness on Junoia to live alone for a month at the age of ten.

Juno smirked. She totally had this.

The floor shook and broke apart under her feet, but still she powered on. Just when Juno thought she was in the clear, a stray rubber ball thwacked her in the head—probably thrown by some kid in the crowd. That was the hazard of doing this sort of thing in front of a live studio audience.

When Juno had agreed to be a competitor on *Fight or Flight*—one of the galaxy's most popular holo-viz broadcasts—she had definitely not expected the obstacle course to be as challenging as it was proving to be. It looked so much simpler when you were watching it from the comfort of your own media room.

Juno adjusted the competitor mask she had been forced to wear (to "make you look fierce," the producers had explained—as if she needed help in that department!). She squinted up at the cameras hovering around her, following her every move. The lights inside the stadium were intense, and it was hard to see past her immediate surroundings. She knew she had to be close to the end of the course, but Juno had no idea how she was doing versus the other competitors. Despite the noisy clanking and whirring of gears and levers all around the stadium, Juno could hear wild applause and cheers from the crowd. For her? Juno hoped so.

Suddenly, all noise stopped. The branches surrounding her went still, and Juno braced herself for the next challenge to swoop in and surprise her. But a moment later, a loud voice rang out over the sound system. "Contestants, we're going to take it from the top again. Camera L is having some technical difficulties, and we missed the whole sequence of Alta running across the bridge. Juno, Alta, Lunddor, Pliz—take five. There are snacks in the *Flight* lounge. We'll call you back to set when we're ready."

Juno gazed up and around, confused. The camera drones buzzed away. She pushed the ridiculous mask up onto her forehead, took a much-needed deep breath of air, and frowned. Pliz, one of the other *Fight or Flight* competitors, strolled past her, whistling. He gave Juno a little salute. "You surviving?"

"Of course," Juno said breezily. She recognized Pliz from past shows—he was a repeat winner of *Fight or Flight*. The round, pockmarked creature looked like a softy, but she knew he would be a tough one to beat. She looked up at the motionless obstacles dangling above her and asked, "What's going on?"

"Snack break," Pliz replied in an unnaturally high

voice. "They always say it will be five minutes, but by the time they redo our makeup and reset the course, it will be more like forty-five. I've been on the show six times now, and it seems like things never run as smoothly as the course directors think they will."

"But—" Juno began. She gazed up at the crowd that had, only moments before, been watching her and the other *Fight or Flight* contestants race through a complicated series of obstacles to try to win the round. Now hundreds of the same fans were eating and milling around and waving to one another. The other two contestants—Alta and Lunddor—were signing autographs for fans at one end of the stadium. Juno fell into step beside Pliz as he made his way toward the *Flight* lounge. "But we hadn't finished that section of the course yet. How can they just stop filming before someone wins? I was almost at the end of the level; I'm sure of it."

Pliz snorted. "Didn't anyone explain how this show works?" He pushed open the door to the *Flight* lounge and grabbed an entire crater cake off the snack table. He stuffed it into his enormous mouth and swallowed the sticky treat without chewing. "I'm going to win."

"I wouldn't be so sure of that if I were you." Juno crossed her arms over her chest. "You're not winning this time, big guy. You have no idea who you're up against."

Pliz let out an enormous burp and flopped down on a

couch. "The show is staged, hon. I don't care how tough you think you are; the producers know the results of this episode before they even start filming. Doesn't matter how bad you want it—my contract says I'll win, so that's what's going to happen."

"The show is staged?" Juno growled. "Like, the whole thing is rigged?"

"Of course," Pliz said. "Now that she's taken over the production, Geela sets it all up herself."

"And you're telling me I'm going to lose?" She squinted at him.

"No matter how hard you fight to get through the course first, they'll figure out a way to throw you off before the end. The results are decided in advance. You never win *Fight or Flight* the first time you're on. That's a guarantee."

Chamberlin poked his head into the *Flight* lounge at that moment. Juno spotted him and glared. She grabbed the curmudgeonly old butler by the arm and pulled him into a corner. "Did you know this show is totally fake? Rigged! Staged!"

"Yes, Your Highness," Chamberlin whispered.

Juno scowled. "You *knew*? I agreed to be on *Fight or Flight* because it would give me a chance to demonstrate my true skills as a warrior. It's not a shampoo commercial, or a singing competition, or any of the fluff the other girls have been asked to be a part of. I want the citizens of the Pentangle Galaxy to see me as something more than just the drummer of a band. I want them to know I'm fierce, and strong, and stealthy—"

Chamberlin cut her off. "If I may . . ." Juno tilted her head to one side, giving him permission to continue. In a shaky voice, Chamberlin went on, "I know you want to prove yourself, Juno. But considering your newfound role in the Resistance, you need to be careful not to attract unwanted attention. Perhaps it isn't such a bad thing if you lose? That will be the best way to continue to keep you hidden in plain sight. Don't you agree?"

Juno considered this. Maybe Chamberlin was right. When the five members of SPACEPOP had been recruited as undercover agents for the Resistance movement against Geela, they had all agreed that rebel missions were a great way to fight back against the horrible creature that had taken over their home planets. But it was essential they never get caught. If any of them was ever caught and then discovered to be not only a member of the Resistance but *also* a princess-in-hiding? It would be a disaster.

So far, no one seemed to suspect that the popular rock band was not just making music but also responsible for some of the Resistance's most important successes. In just a few weeks on the job, the girls had destroyed

Geela's media servers, outfitted the so-called empress's entire fleet of space tankers with tracking devices, and blown up one of her most powerful weapons. The band's "day job" as SPACEPOP was a great disguise for the princesses-in-hiding, but the rock band was also a great cover for their rebel activity. No one would ever suspect the sweet musical group was capable of pulling off much more than a back-to-back set.

But if Juno were to win *Fight or Flight*, she might draw unwanted attention to herself and the others. Still, the athletic princess was proud and didn't want to look like some kind of slowpoke. Juno didn't like to lose—ever. Which meant Pliz wasn't going to win again, not if she had anything to say about it. "No," she announced suddenly. "I want to win this thing."

"Too late," Chamberlin said with a shrug. "Your contract has you coming in second. And as your manager, I get the final word."

Juno slammed her fist down on the table. A platter of tiny Meteor Crunch Bites and a bowl of Crispy Crater Eel Wafers flew into the air. Pliz dove for them, gobbling everything up before it hit the ground. The guy's reflexes were unbelievable! "I don't want to be second," Juno hissed at Chamberlin. "I order you to renegotiate my contract so I can *win*."

Chamberlin heaved a sigh. Juno was one of the least

dramatic of the five princesses, but even she had her moments. Trying to sound commanding, the royal butler said, "I'm afraid the answer is no. Save your anger for Geela, if you must."

"Oh, I will," Juno promised, scowling. "I *definitely* will."

RHEA RAN ONE PALE BLUE HAND OVER AN ELEGANT satin dress, admiring the feel of the cool, smooth fabric on her skin. She gazed down at the dress's designer and watched her as she stitched a sleek leather cape. "Are these pieces meant to go together?" Rhea asked. She could feel the cameras at her back, capturing her every word.

The budding designer—Yaya—looked up and smiled. "I hope so?"

Rhea grinned back at her. "I think you're definitely on the right track, then. I love the contrasting fabrics—the dress is so sweet and delicate, while the cape will give the whole outfit a rough edge."

Yaya breathed a sigh of relief. "Does that mean I'll have your vote during final judging, then?"

Shrugging one shoulder, Rhea gave Yaya a sly wink. When she had signed on to be that week's guest judge on *Galactic Fashion*, Rhea had been ordered to never reveal who would get her vote until it came time for the final judging. So she said coyly, "You'll have to wait and see." But as soon as the cameras had moved away, Rhea mouthed, "Yes! I love it."

Yaya beamed and mouthed back, "Thank you!"

Rhea had been serving as a guest judge on the set of the popular design show for two days. After several very long days of work, the designers were just hours away from the episode's final judging. Rhea knew without a doubt that Yaya was her favorite designer in the competition— by far. Her pieces were edgy and interesting, just like Rhea's own fashion designs. Her use of color and texture was incredible, and Rhea longed to hire Yaya to design something exclusively for her someday. Perhaps when Rhea was back home at the Rhealo palace—going by her full name, Rhealetta Hemmings, again—she could commission Yaya to design her a royal ball gown.

Rhea had always loved wearing pieces that were totally original and a little offbeat, with unique elements like the oversize blue hat she had designed for herself to wear during her stint as a guest judge on *Galactic Fashion*. The hat showcased Rhea's over-the-top, quirky style—and also helped keep the princess-in-disguise's face more hidden from the cameras.

The cameras followed as Rhea strolled past the other designers' pieces, offering her criticism and a few compliments. Everyone on set was working so hard to come up with beautifully designed pieces that would guarantee a chance to sew on for another week. The contestants had just a few minutes remaining to work on stitching their outfits before the models would come in to walk the pieces down the runway for the final judging. There was only one week left in the competition, and whoever was crowned the winner next week would walk away with a huge cash prize.

Ever since she was small, Rhea had longed to serve as a guest judge on *Galactic Fashion*. She'd been a fan of the show for years, but because she had too many royal duties, she had never been allowed to pursue opportunities like this. She didn't have time before, and she knew that having a princess judge the designs would be too intimidating for the competitors.

When SPACEPOP started to get famous, Rhea had finally gotten her chance. It was public knowledge that Rhea designed SPACEPOP's stage outfits, so the producers of *Galactic Fashion* had asked her to come in and film a guest-judging segment. She was having a blast. The designers competing on this season of the show were talented and hardworking, and Rhea admired them all for pursuing their dreams. She couldn't wait to see who would win the whole thing—they all had big plans about what they would do with the money (design school, paying off debt, donating to charity), and any one of them was a deserving winner. Still, Rhea hoped Yaya would take the final trophy. Her talent outshone everyone else's by miles.

Rhea was giving a few tips to one of the most conservative designers when the executive producer of the reality show breezed into the sewing room. She clapped twice, then called for everyone's attention. "Listen up, folks. We have a big surprise for you—major twist!"

All the contestants looked up from their work. The fashion models had just begun to gather at the edges of the room, and the designers were starting to fit their pieces to the models for the final judging.

"Please welcome our newest contestant," the producer said with a grim smile, while the cameras continued to roll. "The beloved empress herself . . . Geela!" She stepped to the side, and a moment later, Geela swept into the room.

Rhea sucked in a breath. "Geela?" she whispered, taking a step back into the shadows. Rhea had been in the same room as the empress only a few times before in her life, and each of those times, she had been undercover on a mission for the Resistance. Rhea tugged her hat down over her face just a bit more, hoping the empress wouldn't notice the similarities between the missing princess of Rhealo and this week's *Galactic Fashion* guest judge.

Like the other four princesses, Rhea had undergone a significant makeover after her escape from the palace— new hair, new clothes, new makeup. But if people were to study her eyes, mouth, or other features up close, they might wonder about SPACEPOP's blue-skinned guitar player. Then again, the self-appointed empress was so self-absorbed that she might not pay Rhea any attention at all.

"That's right, it's true," Geela said, answering the unspoken question everyone wanted to ask. "I am entering one of my own fashion designs into this season's competition. And let me make this very clear: I have every intention of winning *Galactic Fashion!*" The self-appointed empress held up a piece of fabric that was either a very large pair of pants or a very small gown with leg holes. "Isn't it beautiful?"

Rhea cringed. It was anything *but* beautiful. The creation was horrid. She and Yaya shared a private look across the room before the producer announced, "Judges? May I have a word?"

The three regular judges and Rhea all filed out of the

room while Geela traipsed around the sewing room rip-ping up some of the other designers' pieces, spilling coffee on others, and wiping her powdered-sugar-doughnut-covered hands on Yaya's leather cape.

As soon as they were out of earshot, the producer turned to the judges with a serious expression. "You understand what needs to happen here, yes?"

Three of the judges nodded solemnly. Rhea cocked her head and said, "We vote for our favorite?"

The producer stared her down. "Yes." She paused. "But just to confirm . . . who is your favorite?"

"Yaya's dress and cape," Rhea said quickly. "By far the best design of the entire competition. She's got serious talent."

The producer closed her eyes and sighed. "No."

"No?" Rhea said.

"No. Your favorite piece is the one Geela designed."

"It's not."

"Yes, it is."

"It's not. That *thing* she was holding up was awful!"

"When we signed you as a guest judge, I was told you were smart," the executive producer groaned. "But appar-ently you are not. Let me explain this in clear terms: you *must* vote for the empress's design to win, or you will regret it. She is the leader of this galaxy, and that makes her the best at everything she does. Period."

"Are you telling me to *lie?*" Rhea whispered.

"I'm telling you that if you value your life and the lives of my staff, you will do the right thing."

After a brief, weighty pause, Rhea nodded—this wasn't the time or place to fight Geela. But as far as she was concerned, it was the last straw. Geela had imprisoned the royal families, destroyed the planets of the Pentangle, and somehow managed to hold the citizens of their usually peaceful galaxy hostage. Even though Geela didn't need the prize money and had absolutely no talent for design, Rhea would vote for the so-called empress's design because she had no choice. People's lives were on the line, and this was no place for a fight.

But Rhea vowed to herself that Geela wouldn't have the last word. The evil empress might have won that day's fashion battle, but Rhea was sure SPACEPOP and the Resistance would win the war.

HERA

WHILE JUNO PROVED HER STRENGTH AND athletic prowess in the *Fight or Flight* arena, and Rhea showcased her fashion expertise on the set of *Galactic Fashion*, and Luna swished and swung her famous hair to help sell more bottles of Solar Glow, SPACEPOP's bass player, Hera, was using her newfound musical fame to promote a very worthwhile cause.

Hera—once known throughout the galaxy as Princess Herazanna Appleby—was as sweet as moon pie and as gentle as spring rain, and she loved nothing more than helping other creatures of the galaxy find their best life. Whether leading her sisters (that's what she called her fellow princesses) in a guided meditation to relax after a big concert, or taking care of sick and injured animals, or offering a cup of tea to Chamberlin at the perfect moment, Hera loved to see the creatures around her relaxed, happy, and loved. So when she was invited to participate in a celebrity-filled weekend critter-adoption event, she was all too happy to volunteer her time.

"Let's start this event by chanting our individual spirits into group harmony!" The organizer of the critter-adoption event, a bongo drummer called Talak-Talek, stood in the center of a mushroom-shaped stage and lifted his hands into the air. Then he beat the top of his drums gently— *ba-dum, ba-dam, ba-dum, ba-dam*—and hummed. Standing right in front of the stage, Hera swayed and sang along with the rest of the crowd. Her face broke into a smile as she soaked in the atmosphere of love.

The weekend pet festival was jam-packed with celebrities helping to bring attention to the event, and there were plenty of activities to keep people entertained. Poets and authors were scheduled to read aloud from their works-in-progress, impromptu music circles popped up all over the place, and famous yogis (including Hera's all-time favorite, Tranla) led guided yoga practice in different parts of the grounds. But the best part of the whole event was the dozens of "cuddle stations" that had been erected on the grounds, where attendees could snuggle with animals that were hoping to leave with their forever families.

Hera's first official obligation as one of the celebrity attendees was a photo shoot with some of the critters up for adoption. The festival organizers were hoping to use photos of celebrities with the needy animals to inspire more people to adopt a pet. "If you could just hold the little critter up . . . yes, like that, love . . ." A photographer lifted his camera and snapped shot after shot of Hera holding an adorable little kwub-kwub cub. Hera peeked out at the camera from behind the creature's pointy ears, and the photographer clicked away.

The furry little critter burrowed into Hera's flowered shirt and cooed. "You sweet little thing!" she whispered into the kwub-kwub's ear. "We're going to find you the perfect forever home sometime this weekend; I'm just sure of it!"

Hera set the kwub-kwub down and turned to the next homeless pet, a prickly lan. Though the lan was much less fluffy and snuggly than the kwub-kwub, Hera found herself charmed by the little creature. She tucked her hands into a pair of thick gloves and then picked the lan up for her next series of promotional photos. "You're going to make some thick-skinned alien *very* happy," she promised the lan as the photographer got a few great shots.

The next creature in line for Hera's photo shoot was a tentacled creature with giant sticky pads on each of its eleven arms. Hera took a deep breath, then wrapped her arms around the slimy critter. It was beautiful, all pink and yellow, and looked to be in excellent health. Hera knew one of the water-planet inhabitants would surely *love* to adopt such a fine beast!

The critter wrapped two of its tentacles around Hera's head, then three more around her body. When the photographer set up the shot, you could barely see anything more than Hera's eyes peeking out from beneath a mess of slimy arms. She giggled as one of the critter's arms tickled her belly. Two more tentacles tousled her long, curly black hair.

When the photographer was sure he had gotten a good shot, Hera tried to return the creature to its holding tank. But the critter refused to let go. "Now, now," she urged gently. "Let go, you silly thing. I can tell you love hugs, and I'm just sure we're going to find a wonderful home for you, too." The critter wrapped its arms even more tightly around Hera's body. She laughed and said, "I promise that if we don't find you a forever home, I'll take you home myself."

As soon as she said that, someone cleared his throat behind her. Hera spun around and grinned out at Chamberlin from beneath a cluster of tentacles. "Oh, hi, Chamberlin!"

"Hera," Chamberlin began quietly. "We cannot take

on anymore pets. Don't you think we have our hands full caring for the five pets that already live with us onboard the space transport? Think of how crowded your room would be with this, uh . . . adorable creature *and* Roxie." When she heard her name, Hera's beloved pet, Roxie, leaped onto Chamberlin's shoulder and gave him a furry kiss. Chamberlin swatted her away.

A moment later, the four other princesses' pets—Athena's confident Mykie, Luna's sweet Adora, Rhea's silly Springle, and Juno's timid pal Skitter—surrounded Chamberlin. The girls' pets *loved* the royal butler, but, as cute as the five colorful little furballs were, Chamberlin didn't always return their overwhelming affections.

All five royal pets had begged to join Hera at the animal-adoption event for the weekend. After a month on the road, they all needed a chance to run around in open spaces and play with other creatures. The space bus could get rather tight and tense from time to time, so the girls and their pets *all* needed a chance to hang out with new friends and stretch their legs on solid ground once in a while.

"But Chamberlin," Hera said, pushing the sweet and slimy creature's tentacles away from her mouth and eyes. "This little critter has become very attached to me."

"Little?" Chamberlin looked baffled. "That thing is anything *but* little." He tried to pry one of the arms away from Hera's body, but the creature was, indeed, attached. Chamberlin shook his head. "Little or big, no matter *how* attached it has become, the rule is: no more pets."

Hera pouted. "Are you sure?"

"I'm sure. You can cuddle any of these creatures as much as you like while you're here, but your role at this event is finding them homes with *other* families. Their perfect forever home . . . that is not the SPACEPOP tour bus."

"Fine," Hera grumbled. She whispered a few comforting words into the creature's slime-filled ear hole, then gently pulled its many arms away from her body one by one. "Good girl," she cooed.

Within minutes of finishing her photo shoot, the images of Hera holding the homeless pets were uploaded to various news sites, animal-rescue blogs, and the SPACEPOP band home page. SPACEPOP's biggest fan—Bradbury—shared a bunch of the images on his fan vlog, ensuring even more exposure.

Less than an hour later, every last one of Hera's new pals had already been adopted. But the thing no one told her? The evil empress Geela had adopted the tiny kwub-kwub, hoping it would help soften her image . . . which meant Hera's pet-rescue project was *far* from over.

ATHENA

"NONSENSE," ATHENA SAID, TOSSING ASIDE A sheaf of papers. She flicked away a messenger bot, powered down a mail droid, and deleted nearly a dozen messages begging for her support, time, or money. "They want me to do an ad for a cleaning bot, Chamberlin," Athena grumbled. "Ridiculous."

"Indeed," Chamberlin agreed, but he was only half listening. He was too focused on steering the SPACEPOP tour bus through an asteroid field. The nervous butler preferred clear skies and open space roads for travel days, but sometimes the girls' schedule now required him to navigate more dangerous airways. He kept reminding himself that any bumpy airways and ship-squashing asteroids were nothing compared with some of the scary situations he'd found himself in during the princesses' missions for the Resistance. *Those* days were truly terrifying.

"And this," Athena said, holding up a tiny messenger droid as if it might bite her. "This company wants me to be the face of a new makeup line. *Makeup!* Offensive. I'm a singer-songwriter and a keyboard player—what does music have to do with makeup?!"

Athena, the most practical member of SPACEPOP— and the band's unofficial leader—had spent the entire morning riffling through a collection of endorsement and guest-judge offers. Like the rest of the members of the band, Athena had been receiving countless requests to use her newfound celebrity to support products, shows, or events. "A singing-competition judge?" Athena said, scowling as she pressed delete. "After what happened to Rhea on *Galactic Fashion*, there's no way I'm going to risk a run-in with Geela. I'd much rather see Geela on *my* terms."

"Yes, Your Highness," Chamberlin muttered. "Personally, I would prefer not to see Geela at all."

Athena—whose full, royal name was Mettathena Mystos—rolled her eyes. Chamberlin was terrified of the so-called empress and constantly trying to persuade the undercover princesses to give up their role in the Resistance. He insisted that they were putting themselves at unnecessary risk. No matter how many times Athena had explained to him that *someone* had to fight back to save their planets, Chamberlin just couldn't understand why it had to be *them*.

Once she'd gotten through all her other mail, the fair-skinned princess of Athenia pulled open a medium-size packing crate. SPACEPOP's clumsy roadie, Rand, had delivered the package to her in the steering cabin just a few minutes earlier. She carefully lifted off the lid of the crate and peered inside. The box was filled with puffed-up packing materials, protecting something small in the center. "What's this?" she asked, pulling out a gleaming bronze box that was only slightly larger than Athena's two hands held side by side.

Under the box was a letter. Athena scanned it, then threw it aside. "Seriously?" she groaned.

"What is it, Your Highness?" Chamberlin asked, daring to look back over his shoulder for only a moment.

"This takes the prize for most ridiculous offer yet," Athena griped. "This company—Ampersand—wants me to get behind a product called Amp It Up that supposedly helps elevate your music to such a high pitch and volume that you can be heard on another planet." She held up the small bronze box and studied it. "Impossible."

"Is it?" Chamberlin asked.

"Absolutely," Athena said. "This product is tiny! There

is no way it works the way they say it will. But according to this letter, they want me to test the product out with the band, then talk it up in a few interviews. They're hoping to build business through word of mouth." Athena studied the amp from all sides. "Apparently we have to be careful about how we use it, since . . ." Athena trailed off and referred back to the letter. " 'Misuse of the device can cause glass to break and metal to shred.' Sounds like a quality product."

"Sounds dangerous," Chamberlin noted.

"Sounds made-up," Athena said. She tossed the letter aside and groaned, "This is all so foolish. Of course I'm pleased that SPACEPOP is getting so much attention—it will help us get our message of freedom and rebellion out to the galaxy more quickly. But I despise wasting time on nonsense like commercials, trivial holo-viz programs, and junk products. I just want to get on with our mission! We can't keep wasting our precious free time on these side projects. Our newfound fame is getting in the way of our bigger mission. We should be using every spare minute we have to write and rehearse new songs, do more for the Resistance, and build new spy gadgets."

Chamberlin twisted the wheel of the space bus and veered away from an oncoming asteroid. He gritted his teeth. All this talk about Resistance missions, combined with the asteroid field, had made him feel a bit ill. He would give anything to put the ship on autopilot and curl up with a nice book of poetry and a cup of just-hot-enough tea.

"But Athena," Chamberlin said, treading carefully. During their weeks together, the royal butler had slowly learned that all the princesses had a tendency to become even more stubborn when Chamberlin tried to tell them what to do. So he had begun to offer advice without it *sounding* like advice—he liked to pose his advice as questions. "Building more spy gadgets will not get your parents back, right? Do you need to spend time on that activity, or should you focus on other activities?" *Like songwriting*, he added silently.

"You're right, Chamberlin!" Athena said, her face brightening. "Sitting around in the space bus building spy gadgets *won't* help us rescue our parents."

Chamberlin nodded. He hoped Athena would see that *patience* was the best course of action. Waiting patiently, performing some quiet activity, while a brave fellow from the Resistance team rescued the royal families from Geela's Dungeon of Dark Doom—that was the best (and safest) strategy.

Athena narrowed her eyes and stared out the front window of the space bus. Slowly, she said, "What we *need* to do is find our parents. We need to search for Geela's Dungeon of Dark Doom—and when we figure out which planet it's hidden on, we need to rescue our parents ourselves! We can save our parents and our planets and restore peace to the galaxy. Anything else is merely a waste of time and energy and entirely impractical."

Chamberlin gaped at her. He stuttered, "Th-th-that is not what I was saying at all!"

Athena flashed him a small smile. "Maybe not . . . but you helped me figure out our next plan. Thanks for the assist, Chamberlin."

Chamberlin sighed and gripped the space bus controls with shaking fingers. "As always, I am happy to help."

CHAPTER 1

FIVE DARK SHADOWS HUSTLED ALONG A LOW-LIT corridor on the planet of Kantal-ka. Dressed in all black and outfitted with sleek weapons and cleverly disguised spy gear, the five princesses of the Pentangle felt very removed from their former posh lives.

"Psst," Rhea hissed from the back of the line as she and the other girls raced around a corner. "Luna! Can you tie your hair back or something? It's huge—there's no way Geela's security cameras aren't going to spot it. It's almost big enough to warrant a few of its own moons." Luna spun around and glared at Rhea—her hair spun with her. Rhea grinned and wiggled a few fingers in a wave.

Luna's long blond hair was her most prized accessory. She had spent several hours deep conditioning and blow-drying it that morning, to prepare for SPACEPOP's show that night. It had taken days and gallons of expensive creams and tonics, but Luna had finally managed to wash away all remnants of Solar Glow. After weeks of suffering through bad hair days, Luna's locks now looked better than ever. "My hair is a lot less noticeable than your constant yammering and bad jokes," Luna snapped back.

"Can we all just focus on the mission?" Athena asked, shushing them both. "We need to finish our exploration of Kantal-ka, then get out of here. In case anyone has for-gotten, according to the information Captain Hansome sent over this morning, Geela's troops are scheduled to return from their training session in fifteen minutes. And tonight's gig starts in less than two hours. We need to wrap up this search and get out of here. We have another job to get to."

The five girls paused when they reached a T in the cor-ridor. Straight ahead of them stood an imposing, glossy black wall. To their left was a giant archway, leading out into the blue-purple Kantal-ka night; to their right, a closed door. There was no sign of life in either direction. "Which way?" Hera asked, glancing at the others. Without waiting for an answer, she closed her eyes and hummed.

"I'm trying to visualize the correct path," Hera said in a moony voice. "I'm getting a definite left vibe. The night sky is calling to me, telling me we all need to step outside and recharge before moving on."

"Then let's go right," Juno said, moving toward the closed door in the opposite direction. "We don't need to recharge. If we want this mission to be successful, we need to explore every possible wing of Geela's facility here on Kantal-ka. Otherwise, we might miss something that could lead us to our parents. And who knows when we might get back to this planet again."

"Juno's right," Athena agreed. "We need to see what's behind that closed door."

"Behind Door Number One . . ." Rhea said in a funny game show announcer voice. "A new space transport!"

Luna flipped her enormous hair over her shoulder and shushed Rhea. Then the five princesses slipped around the corner and made their way toward the mysterious closed door.

On orders from Resistance leader Captain Hansome, Rhea, Luna, Athena, Hera, and Juno had been exploring Geela's central command station on Kantal-ka for just short of four hours. During that time, they had found no evidence that Geela's Dungeon of Dark Doom was hidden away on the foggy planet of Kantal-ka. But it seemed that every time they thought they had reached the end of the facility, there were more doors leading into unexplored turf.

Athena reached out to press a button, and the closed door whooshed open. They all slipped through the door and waited as it closed behind them. Ahead of them stretched another long, empty corridor that led to yet another door. The girls raced down the corridor, pressed another button, and this door slid open. On the other side of this door was yet *another* long corridor with yet another door at the far end. The girls carried on. And on. And on.

"What's with all the doors?" Rhea asked after they had passed through the sixth identical door. "Think Geela's just really into climate control or something?"

Juno narrowed her eyes. When she was a contestant on *Fight or Flight*, she had faced a maze of doors and hallways that felt eerily similar to the one they were in now. Her stomach clenched into a fist and she muttered, "I hope it's not some kind of trap. These doors must be protecting something."

Rhea scanned the smooth walls, searching for security cameras or any other indication that someone might be watching their every move in some far-off control room. She couldn't find any signs of enhanced security or tracking devices, which made her think they were on a wild-goose chase. "Has anyone else considered the fact that none of these doors are locked? And we haven't seen a single guard or one of Geela's Android Soldiers all day. If the Dungeon of Dark Doom was hidden somewhere in this facility on Kantal-ka, don't you think it would be better protected?"

The other girls nodded their agreement. But until they were absolutely *sure* they had hit a dead end, none of them was willing to call off the search. Because when—*if?*—they found Geela's Dungeon of Dark Doom, the girls were sure they would also find their imprisoned parents. That singular goal was propelling them all forward, giving them strength to carry on with their difficult and dangerous Resistance mission. If they could find the secret location of Geela's Dungeon of Dark Doom, they would be able to release their parents, thus allowing the Pentangle Galaxy—and its princesses—to go back to life as usual.

Thanks to intelligence the girls had helped gather on one of their first assignments for the Resistance (the SPACEPOP crew planted trackers on Geela's entire fleet of space tankers), Captain Hansome and his team had been able to figure out that Geela and her army spent the majority of their time and resources on five planets— Kantal-ka, Lud, Pallomo, Tik-tik, and Pluton. By using the tracker data the disguised princesses had helped to collect, Resistance forces decided to turn their attention to these five planets to see if they could figure out how to weaken Geela's strongholds.

When Hansome told the girls about the team's findings, Athena was the one who pointed out that it would also make sense to narrow the search for the missing royal families to those five planets. Geela was the kind of leader who would enjoy visiting her prisoners regularly, relishing in their discomfort and weakness. She wouldn't be likely to hide the Dungeon of Dark Doom anywhere that would be too hard for her to reach or too remote for her to visit regularly. Therefore, if Resistance forces were to conduct an extensive search of each of the five planets Geela spent most of her time on, they would very likely find the hidden Dungeon of Dark Doom *and* the royal prisoners.

The trouble was, each of the five planets the Resistance forces needed to search was in strict lockdown mode. All travel onto and off each of the planets was restricted, and the only way anyone was allowed in the planets' airspace was with a valid travel authorization. Anyone caught entering or leaving without said authorization would be destroyed without question. So it wasn't as simple as dispersing Resistance forces to search each planet in a hurry—no one could land on any of these planets to start the hunt.

When Captain Hansome had delivered the bad news,

Luna shrugged. "So we use our cover as SPACEPOP to get the necessary travel authorizations."

Hansome stared at her blankly for a moment, and then his eyes brightened on the holo-screen communicator. "Yes!" he cried. He flung his muscled green arms up into the air and pumped his fists. Luna swooned at the sight of his strapping muscles. She had a major *thing* for Captain Hansome, but the Resistance leader didn't seem to return her affections. The handsome captain was so caught up in his own awesomeness that he didn't have time to flirt back. "Luna, you are absolutely right."

"I am?" Luna squeaked. The self-confident princess only ever lost her cool in front of Captain Hansome. But after a moment of wide-eyed blinking, she gathered her wits, then splashed an enormous smile across her face. "I mean—yeah, I guess I am."

"If you book a concert or . . . gig? Is that what you call them, gigs?"

"Yeah," Rhea said, rolling her eyes.

Hansome stroked his chin. Luna sighed dramatically when he flicked a braided lock of hair off his forehead. The strapping Resistance captain went on, "If you book SPACEPUP gigs on the five planets we need to gain access to, it will give you the perfect cover. You can slip in and out without attracting notice."

"Um," Rhea muttered. "The point of a *gig* is to attract

attention. We're not going for empty stadiums here, y'know. It's kind of hard to spread our message of peace, love, and rebellion if no one's listening."

Juno growled, "And it's SPACE*POP*, bub. Not SPACE*PUP*."

"Of course, of course." Hansome laughed his gruff belly laugh, which made Luna swoon—again. The miniature holo-version of the captain patted his blue-and-pink Mohawk into place and adjusted his worn leather vest over his muscled chest. "I just mean, if you secure clearance to enter these planets for your band stuff, you won't be calling attention to yourselves as *spies*. You'll garner plenty of attention for your cute little songs, of course."

The girls exchanged irritated looks. Hansome was constantly dismissing their band as fluff and failing to realize the impact their successful missions had had on his precious Resistance. They had destroyed Geela's servers and taken down her whole media empire! Yet he never gave them the credit they were due. Whenever they reported back to him after a mission, he would scold them for not following his orders to the letter, write off their successes as lucky breaks, or take credit for the results himself. Someday, the princesses hoped, he would realize just how useful they were . . . to him, and to the Pentangle Galaxy.

It took a little convincing and creativity in scheduling, but Chamberlin had managed to book the girls a gig on

Kantal-ka. It was only a small auditorium show—not the huge arenas the band preferred to play in now that they had achieved a certain level of fame—but the small gig was enough to secure the band's clearance to enter Kantal-ka airspace. They had arrived on the fog-covered planet that morning. Moments after they landed, the girls slipped into their rebel gear and left Chamberlin and Rand—the band's innocent roadie—to prep for their gig that afternoon while they were off on their reconnaissance mission.

"Another door?" Rhea groaned as the spies made their way down yet another unmarked hallway. "How big *is* this place?"

"And where do all these doors lead?" Athena wondered.

When they hustled through the ninth door, all five girls screeched to a stop . . . narrowly avoiding plunging off a narrow catwalk into a bottomless black abyss. They were standing at the edge of a huge, cavernous room. A narrow walkway snaked around the perimeter of the room, overlooking inky black nothingness. Suddenly, Luna shrieked and pointed.

The others followed her finger. There, shivering on a small, floating disc in the center of the room—surrounded on all sides by open air and empty space—were Chamberlin and Captain Hansome.

CHAPTER 2

CHAMBERLIN LIFTED HIS HAND IN A TIMID WAVE. "Greetings."

"Chamberlin?" Athena said, squinting. "Captain Hansome?"

"It is us!" Captain Hansome said in a blustery voice. "Hello!"

"Uh, hello?" Luna squeaked. She shook her hair around her shoulders and squeezed her cheeks to give them a little color.

"What are you doing way out there?" Juno asked. "And how did you *get* there?"

"Bit of a situation," Chamberlin began. "You see, the captain and I were coming to—"

Hansome cut him off and blurted out, "To rescue you!"

Rhea snorted. "Mighty fine job you've done of it, too."

Captain Hansome flexed his muscles and put his arm around Chamberlin in a chummy sort of way. The move nearly knocked the old guy off the narrow platform. The royal butler sunk to his knees, his breath wheezing out in a giant whoosh as he held the edges of the floating disc for dear life. "Yes, well," Captain Hansome said in a bold voice. "When you didn't return at the time we were expecting you, I grew concerned for your safety. So I gathered up old Chamberlin here—who insisted he come along, the brave old chap!—and we entered Geela's facility to help you girls out. Figured you could use a hand."

"You came to help us?" Athena put her hands on her hips and said plainly, "Looks like you're the ones who need the help."

Captain Hansome chuckled. "Yes, well, about that . . ." Hansome lost his footing as the outer edge of the platform he and Chamberlin were standing on broke away and fell—soundlessly—into the bottomless pit. The disc was now much smaller and obviously even harder to balance on. Hansome peered over the edge of his little island and spoke more quickly. "While we were searching for you, we came upon this room. As we were racing across the middle of the floor—toward that door, there—"

Captain Hansome cut off and gestured to a small door on the other side of the room. "All of a sudden the floor below us began to fall away. First the far edges broke apart, then more and more. Within seconds, we were left on this small platform . . . and our resting spot seems to be getting smaller every minute. Perhaps this room is under construction and we weren't meant to walk here?"

"I highly doubt the room is under construction," Athena said, lifting one eyebrow. "But I think you're right about one thing: we're not meant to be here."

Hera nodded. "This must be Geela's way of ensuring no one gets past this room. No need for guards when you can trap someone in the middle of a bottomless pit, am I right?" The others stared at her. Hera was sweet, kind, and caring—and had been known to keep the other girls from driving one another crazy, or worse, more than a few times—but she was usually not the member of the group who figured things out first. "What?" Hera asked. "Geela must have had some sort of motion detectors set up in the room so if anyone tried to cross over to the next door, they would be trapped with nowhere to go."

"Exactly," Juno said, nodding. "Well said, Hera."

"Thanks!" Hera chirped.

"What I still don't get," said Rhea, "is why you thought we needed your help getting out of here. We've proved ourselves to be capable, resourceful, and safe in every one of our missions for . . . *the Resistance* . . ." Rhea said the word *Resistance* the way Captain Hansome always did—with emphasis. None of the girls tired of making fun of him behind his back for the way he accentuated *Resistance*. It was the band's little inside joke.

Athena jumped in. "Might I remind you, we are the team that secured clearance to enter the Kantal-ka airspace and we were perfectly comfortable executing this mission on our own."

"With no 'help' from you," Juno added, putting the word *help* in little quotation marks.

"Perhaps we could talk more about the *hows* and *whys* of this, uh, *little* situation after we've found a way to get ol' Chamberlin to more solid ground?" Hansome suggested.

"Fair enough," Rhea said, smirking. "Can you say the magic words?"

"M-m-magic words?" Captain Hansome stuttered as more of the platform broke away. The tiny island that was keeping Chamberlin and Hansome from certain doom was now just barely large enough to fit the two men. "What are the magic words?" It was the first time any of the girls had seen Captain Hansome ruffled. But it didn't take a genius to figure out that soon there would be room left for only one of them on the disc.

"Pretty please," Rhea began slowly. While she spoke, she scanned the perimeter of the room. Her face split into a smile when she spotted a control panel directly across from where the girls were standing. Rhea had a knack for programming that came in handy at times like this. She glanced at Captain Hansome again and, in a deep voice that sounded nothing like the strapping captain's, said, "Pretty please, Resistance rock stars, will you rescue us?"

"Rescue *me*?!" Captain Hansome said, chortling. "Might I remind you, I am here to rescue you girls—not the other way around!" But the arrogant captain stopped laughing when yet another chunk of the platform broke away. His foot slipped off the edge of the platform, and Hansome screamed like a crater eel. "Pretty please!" he shrieked. "Pretty please, help us out of here!"

"Attaboy," Juno said. "Nicely done."

As Rhea raced around the edge of the room toward the control panel, Luna pulled out a plain-looking can of hair spray. She shook it and then sprayed the aerosol can into the empty space between the perimeter walkway and the floating disc. The misty spray illuminated a web of red laser beams, crisscrossing the space between the walkway and the floating disc. "Motion sensors," she said, glancing at Athena. "You were absolutely right, Hera."

"Yippee!" Hera cheered. Her dark curls bounced around her face as she fumbled around in the slim pocket of her black spy suit. Gleefully, she pulled out a tube of lipstick, held it up to her lips, and called out, "Come in, Athena. Athena, do you copy?"

Juno snatched the lipstick out of Hera's hand. "Not the right time, Hera. Save your lipstick communicator for sometime when you're *not* standing right at Athena's side. You're supposed to use it for communicating from afar, remember?"

Hera pouted and glanced from Juno to Athena. "But Luna got to use the cool laser-detector hair spray Athena made for her. I want to use some of my spy gadgets, too! The only thing I have on me is my lipstick communicator . . ."

"Here." Athena tossed her what looked like an ordinary pair of reading glasses. "Put these on—if anyone from Geela's team shows up while we're trying to free these two, you can look them in the eye and hypnotize them. The effects will wear off after just a minute—I'm still working on that part—but it will buy us some time. The hypno-glasses are still in early development, so I'm not sure if they'll work quite like they're supposed to."

"Ooh!" Hera said, bouncing happily. "Fun!" She put the glasses on and looked at Juno. "How do they look?"

"Hera!" Athena snapped. "Don't look at any of *us*. You don't want to hypnotize anyone on your own team."

Hera nodded solemnly and looked down at the ground. "Right! Sorry!"

"We need to figure out some way to deactivate the sensors before we get them off the platform," Athena said, thinking aloud. She tugged a length of rope out of her suit, tying one end into a secure knot. "If we can deactivate the sensors, we can swing this rope over and pull them both to safety."

"Pull?" Chamberlin moaned, his face pale. "Swing?" He closed his eyes and took deep breaths. "Might I remind you, I am *far* too old for this nonsense. I don't do ropes. Period."

Across the way, Rhea had bashed open the front of the control panel, and she was expertly twisting at wires and cords inside. She snipped a length of wire, and another half of the floating disc broke away. "Oopsie," she said, cringing as the two men huddled more closely together. "Wrong wire. But we're almost there," she called. "The lasers should be deactivated in a minute. Just give me a second . . . I think I figured out which wire controls the platform, at least. It shouldn't get any smaller, so you guys are safe there for now." She gave Hansome and Chamberlin a thumbs-up sign.

While they waited for Rhea to work her programming magic, Juno stared out over the web of red lasers, furrowing her brow. She cocked her head to one side and said, "Does anyone else see a pattern in the lasers?"

Athena, Luna, and Hera all gazed out at the

crisscrossing red lines, trying to figure out what Juno was talking about. Juno had an artist's eye, a flair for graphic design and the way lines and shapes worked together, so she often noticed things the other girls didn't.

"It's Geela's face," Juno said, pointing. "There's her eye, and her chin, and right there—her hair, all swept up in a crazy bun. She turned her own laser motion detectors into a sort of art, honoring herself."

The other three girls gasped. "You're right!" Just as soon as the laser outline of Geela's face was burned into each of their minds, the red lines flickered and went out.

"Ta-da!" Rhea said, pumping her fist on the other side of the room. "Motion detectors off. Commence rescue mission."

"I'd like the record to show," began Captain Hansome in a blustery voice, "that we would have figured out a way out of here *without* your help. Things were going according to plan. I was just about to save Chamberlin when you breezed into the room."

"Is that so? Shall we leave you there to figure it out, then?" Rhea asked. "I wouldn't want to damage your hero card by helping you out of a sticky situation. We need to get back to the space bus to prepare for our gig tonight, so if you think you're all set here, then we'll just leave you to it!"

Captain Hansome smiled. "Now, now. As long as

you're here, we might as well all leave together. No sense in you girls getting lost on the way out."

Athena looked at her bandmates. Without their exchanging a single word, she could tell they were all in agreement. "Here's the deal, Captain Hansome," she said in her serious, clipped voice. "If we get you out of here, you promise to start treating us as important members of this team. No more following us to make sure we're safe. If we rescue you from that platform, from now on you give us your full respect and nothing less. Do we have a deal?"

The Resistance captain cocked his head to one side. One corner of his mouth quirked up into a half smile. "Let's not be silly . . ." he began.

On the other side of the cavernous room, Rhea fiddled with a wire. Another chunk of the floating disc broke away and left Hansome clinging to Chamberlin for support. "Oops," she said, shrugging.

Captain Hansome gritted his teeth. "It's a deal. Pretty please rescue me, and you'll have my undying respect."

Athena beamed. "Good boy."

CHAPTER 3

AS SOON AS HANSOME AND CHAMBERLIN WERE back on solid ground, they all raced around the catwalk and made their way toward the closed door on the far side of the cavernous room. If Geela had gone to so much trouble to protect whatever she was hiding with that series of doors, corridors, and a breakaway floor, there *must* be something good tucked away.

The band, Chamberlin, and Captain Hansome had only a few minutes left to explore the rest of the facility, for any minute now, the Android Soldiers would return from their training session. None of them wanted to be around for that. Geela's henchmen were huge, metal beasts with no conscience whatsoever, and their only hope of survival was avoiding an encounter with the soldiers altogether. They had timed their exploration to coincide with the army's daily training session and oil dip (a design flaw required the Android Soldiers to take an oil bath daily to keep their metal shells from rusting).

Rhea, who had already made it to the other side of the bottomless pit to mess around with the wires inside the control panel, got to the mystery door first. She pressed a button to open it. Unlike all the other doors they had encountered in their exploration of Kantal-ka, this one didn't budge. "Locked," she said.

"Ah, well," muttered Chamberlin. "Guess we might as well be on our way, then?"

"Not a chance," Rhea grunted, fiddling with the metal plate around the door. "I just need to jimmy this wire and—" She broke off as the door whooshed open. Shaking her head, she said, "Geela's security is not impressive." Rhea covered her mouth to hold in a laugh as she stepped into the room. "No. Way."

"What is it?" Luna asked, hustling forward for a look. She squeaked with glee when Hansome leaned against her shoulder to gaze past her into the room. The space on the other side of the door was at least a hundred feet high. The walls were curved, making the space feel almost like the turret of an old-fashioned castle from Earth the girls had seen in faded paper photographs. In the center of the room stood an enormous gilded mirror.

Captain Hansome rubbed his stubbly chin as he studied the contents of the room. Perplexed, he asked the others, "Are those . . . dead creatures lining the walls?"

This was enough to send Rhea into a fit of laughter. Hera, on the other hand, broke into sobs. The idea of a room lined with dead critters was enough to crush her spirit for days.

"They're not dead critters," Luna said, stepping forward to touch one of the furry-looking things hanging from the wall. "This room is filled with wigs."

"Wigs?!" Athena snapped.

Beside her, Hera perked up. "Not critters?"

Luna ran her hands over the mounds and mounds of hair that lined the walls. "Definitely not critters. These are high-quality wigs. Hundreds of them."

"Geela's?" Juno said, snickering. "The Dark Empress of Evil wears *wigs*?"

Before they could consider this glorious new information, a high-pitched alarm rang out in the building. A mechanical voice droned, "All units, report for duty!"

"We've got to go," Juno said, her muscles tensing as she went on high alert. "The guards are coming back."

"This way!" Hansome called, beckoning the girls to follow him. "I'll lead you out."

"Oh, no you don't," Athena said, stepping in front of him. "With all due respect, Captain, please follow us this time. This is our mission, and success or failure needs to rest on our shoulders."

"Before we go . . ." Rhea whispered, nudging Luna. She turned back to look into the room full of wigs. "I think I'll just leave Geela a little parting gift." She reached into her pocket, pulled out a stink bomb, and let it fly high into the center of all that hair.

Luna high-fived her, giggling. "Not even Solar Glow can wash away that odor."

"Indeed." Rhea laughed. "Bad hair days begone? Nope. I foresee a few stinky hair days in Geela's future."

Less than a half hour later, the SPACEPOP crew was back in the space bus. As soon as they knew the group was safe and sound and hadn't been tracked, Hansome excused himself to the bus's control room, eager to transmit details of the Kantal-ka exploration back to Resistance Headquarters. But before he escaped to gloat about his extreme bravery and stealth, Juno asked him, "Captain Hansome: How, exactly, did you manage to get onto this restricted planet in the first place?"

"I snuck onto your bus," he said, shrugging. He wiggled

his fingers in front of his face and announced, "Master of disguise!" He bowed, then hustled away.

The girls headed toward their sleeping quarters and common room.

"That guy," Juno grumbled as she crossed the common room to get to her sleeping pod.

Luna sighed dreamily. *"That guy."* She gazed at herself in the giant mirror in the center of the girls' common room. Smiling, she twisted her hair up, then let it cascade around her shoulders again. *"That guy . . ."*

Hera snuck up behind her and snapped a picture. "Act natural," she instructed.

"What are you doing?" Luna demanded, grabbing the camera to inspect the photo. She scowled and deleted it before Hera had a chance to protest.

"Bradbury suggested we get more candid shots of the band 'behind-the-scenes' for the SPACEPOP website," Hera explained. "He said he talked to you about it."

"He did," Luna said, pushing her lips out into a sweet pout. She squeezed her cheeks to give them a little extra golden color and shook her hair out until it was as big as possible. "Ready!" she said, beaming at Hera.

"That's not candid," Hera said, frowning. "You're all posed."

"I am *not*," Luna insisted. "I look awful. No lipstick or

anything! This is *so* behind-the-scenes and candid I'm practically grotesque."

"I've seen you first thing in the morning," Rhea said under her breath. She peeked around the corner of her own sleeping pod, half-dressed in her performance outfit. "*That* is grotesque."

Luna threw a tube of lipstick across the room. Hera snapped a quick photo just as Rhea ducked back inside her room to hide. While Luna continued to primp, Hera turned her attention to the pile of pets snoozing on the floor of the girls' common room. When the girls were first introduced, none of the princesses' pets had seemed excited about sharing his or her beloved owner with four other critters. But after just a few hours of sniffing and snuffing at one another, the five cuddly pets had become fast friends. Now they spent much of the day napping in a furry pile of mixed-up colors. The little critters loved to get up and dance while the girls rehearsed, and they were often invited along on Resistance missions to help in their own special way—each of the girls' pets had strange quirks that made her useful from time to time.

Hera crept forward and snapped a close-up of the snoozing pet pile. Juno's shy pet, a purple fluffball called Skitter, opened one eye and burrowed deeper inside her pile of friends to hide from the camera. Rhea's pet, a quirky blue critter called Springle, bounced out of the pile and knocked the camera out of Hera's hands. Giggling, Hera fell over onto the floor and let the soft collection of pets jump on her and tickle her until she cried, "Peace! Peace!"

"Hera, you better start getting ready," Luna called out from in front of the mirror. "One hour until we go on."

Hera scooped up an armful of fluffy pets and rubbed their soft fur against her face. "Oh, I'm ready."

"Really?" Luna said, cocking an eyebrow. "Are you going to do something about your hair? It's all frizzy from wrestling with the animals."

Rhea peeked out of her room again. Chuckling, she burst out, "Or maybe you could wear one of Geela's wigs onstage?"

Luna and Hera both cracked up along with her. Hera draped her own pet—a feisty pink critter named Roxie—across the top of her head and pretended she was wearing a wig. This made Luna and Rhea laugh even harder. Though the five princesses fought like real sisters much of the time, the group also had a lot of fun together. It helped that each girl had a small sleeping pod she could decorate in her own personal style. When one of them needed a break from the others to rest, relax, or (in the case of Hera) meditate, she could escape to her pod and sink into a space that felt safe and somewhat like home.

The space bus was small and cramped compared with the palaces and grand homes the five princesses were all accustomed to living in, but it had been smartly designed to make the most of a small amount of space. There was a common living room in the center of the transport; Chamberlin had a small private room near the transport's only bathroom; and the band's roadie, Rand, slept hanging upside down in a minuscule supply closet whenever he needed to catch a few Zs (which was not often, as the four-armed alien came from a planet with very long days and almost no night). At the far back end of the space bus were the girls' quarters, which had been broken into the five individual sleeping pods connected by a small living room that the girls used for hanging out, writing songs, and planning their missions.

Now Athena stepped out of her private pod wearing her performance outfit for that night's show. With only a quick glance in the mirror, she swept some lipstick over her lips and then settled down at her keyboard with a look of extreme concentration on her face. She and Luna had been working on writing a new song together for the past week or so, but they hadn't gotten far. Band business had gone a little off-track while they'd prepped for their mission to search for the Dungeon of Dark Doom on Kantal-ka. "Anyone want to jam to warm up for tonight?" she asked. "I'm totally stuck on this new song. We're going to need to drop a new hit soon to keep people excited about SPACEPOP, or we'll be last week's news."

Luna glanced at Athena in the mirror and waved her off. "You can't rush greatness," she told her. "True creative inspiration strikes when the time is right."

"I disagree," Athena said pointedly. "I believe great songs come from a place of hard work, not luck."

"That's where we differ," Luna said, lining her lips in color. "Songs need to come from your heart. The words won't arrive until they're ready. You can't force them to appear."

The other three girls and their pets swung their heads back and forth, watching the disagreement with great interest. Athena and Luna were about as different from each other as two girls could be, but when they wrote songs together, the result was almost always incredible. Luna had a true ear for how words fit together and—as she often pointed out—a singing voice that was second to none. Athena's discipline and strict musical training gave her the perfect background for composing.

"Your Highnesses," Chamberlin said, stepping into the girls' common room just before the argument escalated any further. "Pardon the interruption, but I have news."

"Ooh, news!" Luna said. "Fan mail?"

"No, not fan mail," Chamberlin said. "Actually,

perhaps it is something like fan mail. Just not the kind you might be hoping for. We've had a message."

"Is it about our parents?" Juno said hopefully, stepping out of her room. Juno and Hera were closer to their parents than any of the other princesses. Athena and Luna both loved their parents, of course, but their relationships were a bit more distant and formal than Juno's and Hera's. Rhea didn't know her parents at all. She had spent her early years in an orphanage, learning about her royal heritage only when she was six—so the king and queen of Rhealo were not her actual parents but connected to her distantly by ancient blood. "Have you received some message from them?"

"I'm sorry, no." Chamberlin cleared his throat, a nervous tic. "I've had a message from the empress's live entertainment network. The band Arion IV has had to cancel their performance on *The Geela Hour* tomorrow night. The producers are looking for a backup band, and they've asked me—your, uh, manager—if you would be willing."

"To perform live in front of millions of galaxy fans?" Luna shrieked. "Oh my Grock! Obviously, the answer is—"

"No," Juno snapped, cutting her off. "We are not going to support one of Geela's shows. I'm not singing for that beast or anyone who works for her. Absolutely not."

Hera held up a hand. "It would be great exposure. And Arion IV is our biggest competition for the slot at the top of the charts, so it would be fun to take their place and make them regret canceling."

"We could perform 'Unstoppable,'" Rhea added. "We've only had the chance to play it at a few shows, and this would be a great opportunity to debut it for a larger audience. It's ready for a bigger stage."

"Rhea and Hera are right," Athena said. "It *is* great exposure. We've never had an audience this size. And the more people who have a chance to hear our songs— especially one like 'Unstoppable'—the more we're doing the job we set out to do of spreading our message of peace, freedom, and rebellion to the rest of the galaxy."

Juno glared at each of the other princesses. "Seriously?"

"Besides, the last thing we need to do is make ourselves targets for Geela by saying no," Athena pointed out.

"Fine," Juno said. "But I'm not smiling during the shoot. Not once."

Rhea grinned. "Not even if we bump into Geela in the hall and I pull the wig right off her horrible head?"

Juno fought against it, but eventually the smile snuck out. "If that happens, *maybe* I'll smile. But no promises."

CHAPTER 4

NO THANKS TO SOLAR GLOW, I'M READY FOR MY HOLO-VIZ CLOSE-UP! LIGHTS, CAMERA, **LUNA!**

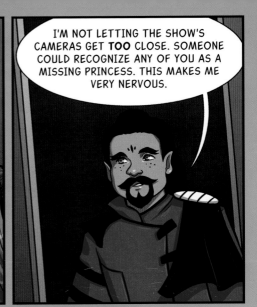

I'M NOT LETTING THE SHOW'S CAMERAS GET **TOO** CLOSE. SOMEONE COULD RECOGNIZE ANY OF YOU AS A MISSING PRINCESS. THIS MAKES ME VERY NERVOUS.

DOUGHNUTS MAKE YOU NERVOUS, CHAMBERLIN. RELAX.

I'LL RELAX WHEN THIS IS ALL OVER AND YOU ARE SAFELY HOME IN YOUR PALACES AGAIN.

I COULD LEAD YOU IN SOME DEEP-BREATHING EXERCISES TO CALM YOU DOWN, IF YOU LIKE!

IF ANYTHING GOES WRONG TONIGHT, **MILLIONS** OF GALAXY RESIDENTS WILL SEE OUR MISTAKES UP CLOSE AND IN REAL TIME!

I STILL THINK GOING ON THIS SHOW IS A **TERRIBLE** IDEA.

MURP!

69

AFTER A ROUGH START, THE GIRLS' PETS JUMPED IN WITH SOME BEATBOXING MAGIC! AND SPACEPOP ROCKED IN A WHOLE NEW WAY.

WE'VE GOT THIS ONE MOMENT. ONE SHOT TO GO ALL THE WAY!

TSS TA-TSS TA-TSSS!

AND WE'RE NOT GONNA LET ANYONE STOP US. ONE VOICE, TOGETHER!

SPLLLT!

WE'RE UNSTOPPABLE! TURN IT UP . . .

REE-ROWR!

. . . 'CAUSE WE ARE READY FOR ANYTHING!

BA-BOW-WOW-WOW!

?!

BRAVA! BRAVA!

OMG!

WE LOVE YOU, SPACEPOP!

YAY!

SO CUTE!

AW!

THAT WAS BRILLIANT!

WITH THAT PERFORMANCE, YOU JUST PROVED THAT YOU DESERVE THE TITLE OF THE NEXT GALACTIC SUPERSTARS! YOU ARE **UNSTOPPABLE**, SPACEPOP!

CHAPTER 5

"SO TELL ME, SPACEPOP . . ." THE BAND HAD JUST wrapped their set, and now Tam, the charming late-night host of *The Geela Hour*, leaned across his enormous glossy desk to begin his interview with the five girls. He spoke to them in a low, conspiratorial voice. "What's your secret?"

"Secret?" Luna squeaked, tugging her bouffant of hair over one half of her face. She and the other girls exchanged nervous looks. What did Tam know? For a brief moment, Luna regretted agreeing to do the live after-show TV interview. The band could have easily made some excuse about needing to hustle off set to hit the space highway to make it to their next gig, but *no*.

Someone (maybe, possibly even Luna herself) had insisted that they needed the publicity and should go ahead and take the interview. "Wh-what secret?"

Tam laughed and pounded his chair. "The secret to your success! How do you do it? Tell me everything!"

"Oh," Rhea said, laughing nervously. "*That* secret."

Tam's eyebrows flew up. "Are there *other* secrets I should know about?"

"None," Athena snapped, cutting him off before the host pressed further. "I'll begin, if that's all right?" Tam nodded, encouraging her to go on. Athena rested her chin in her hand, trying to spread her fingers so they would cover as much of her face as possible. Unlike Rhea, who often wore a hat, and Luna, who had all that hair to hide behind—she, Juno, and Hera had to be extra careful in front of the cameras. She turned toward Tam so the cameras would be able to capture only her profile. She took a deep breath, hoping for the best. "I am confident the secret to our success is this: we truly believe in the songs we sing. Our music imparts a message each one of us feels strongly about. Additionally, we've all had extensive musical training—"

Tam cut her off, his enormous eyes practically bulging out of his slim head. "Is that so? Tell me more!"

"Oh," Athena said, realizing a little too late that most nearby galaxies didn't offer extensive music education to anyone. Music lessons were usually a privilege reserved for the very rich—or royal. The SPACEPOP girls hadn't ever gone into a lot of detail about their backgrounds with reporters, obviously, and none of them wanted to get into it now. "Well, by that I don't mean . . . or rather . . . uh . . ." For once, Athena was flustered.

Juno broke in, hoping to shift the focus away from the girls' lives before SPACEPOP. "I think what Athena is trying to say is not that we've had extensive *professional* training, but that we've all worked hard to perfect our craft because we just love to make music. It wasn't simple to figure out what works, but now here we are. The most important thing the galaxy should know is, we work well together. It's not always easy to get along as a group of five, but it's essential to making the band work."

Tam nodded. "Together, eh? So do you write your songs as a group?"

"Mostly, yes," Athena said, finally recovering.

"That's not true!" Hera cut in, her black curls bobbing around her face as she smiled merrily. "They're both too modest to admit it, but the truth is Luna and Athena usually take the lead. The rest of us chime in from time to time with a few lines, but they're both really talented when it comes to songwriting."

"Aha!" said Tam. "So the truth comes out! So are you saying Athena and Luna are the leaders of the band?"

Luna—who had never before been accused of modesty—nodded vigorously, while Athena frowned and shook her head. Luna glanced over at her songwriting partner and stopped nodding. "We all play an equal part in this band," Athena said curtly. "We don't have a leader."

"Except Chamberlin!" Rhea chimed in, a mischievous grin on her face. "Our manager, of course."

"Chamberlin," Tam said, stroking his chin. "I wanted to speak with you about him. He's an unusual choice for a manager. No previous experience in the industry, but he seems to be doing an impressive job ushering you girls into the limelight." The host leaned forward and whispered, "I hope you're paying him enough, or some other band may snatch him up."

"Oh, I highly doubt that," Rhea said.

"Moving on!" Tam burst out suddenly, apparently done talking about Chamberlin. "Tell us more about your lives *before* SPACEPOP. The universe wants to know everything. Any fun stories about the girls *behind* the legends?"

"Legends?" Rhea said with a grin, cocking an eyebrow. "Really, Tam? Let's not get ahead of ourselves."

Hera raised her hand. "I'll take this one, if I may?" She glanced at her bandmates for approval. They all reluctantly nodded, unsure of how Hera would answer the question. "I'm sure everyone has figured out by now that I love animals. All critters—big or small, slimy or soft—are dear to my heart, and most of my stories from childhood involve me playing outside with pets or wild creatures. But here's something you probably *don't* know about me: I absolutely love moonberry crackle! And one of my fondest memories from childhood is sneaking into the kitchen to steal spoonfuls of the batter before the cooks—"

"Cooks?" Tam burst in.

"M-my mother!" Hera said, recovering quickly with a small white lie. "My mother and her friends loved to cook together. They always asked me to call them Cook when they were in the kitchen."

"That's very sweet," Tam said. "And itty-bitty Hera would sneak into the kitchen and snatch a taste?"

"That's right," Hera said. She laughed. "But once, I was too greedy and I accidentally knocked over the whole pod of batter. I can still remember the look on my mother's face when she saw me sitting there on the floor sur- rounded by a sugary-sweet mess." Suddenly, Hera stopped talking. Her eyes filled with tears. She missed her par- ents terribly and longed for the day when she would see them again.

Tam smiled sympathetically, then asked, "Do you get back to see your families often, or does your tour sched- ule keep you too busy for family?"

"We're working on a trip to see our parents right now," Juno said. "It's tough to find the time, but if our plan—er, schedule—works out, we should reunite with them soon."

"Wonderful, wonderful," Tam said.

"I have a story, too!" Luna said, realizing she hadn't been in the spotlight nearly enough—and also that her contract with Solar Glow required that she mention the product whenever she was doing interviews. "So when I was very young, I didn't know how to manage my hair. It's naturally wavy and very, very thick."

"May I?" Tam asked, smirking as he reached out a long-fingered hand to touch Luna's hair.

"Of course," Luna giggled, holding a clump of her hair in his direction. "Well, I used to get the most awful tangles. The palace—"

"Palace?"

Luna's fair skin grew even paler as she blinked at Tam. "That's a little joke my parents and I shared. We used to call our home the palace, to make it feel more spacious than it actually was."

Tam grinned out at the studio audience. "How sublime!"

Luna chewed her lip. She gave Tam a *look*, and then said, "May I continue?" He nodded, and she went on. "One morning, I woke up and my hair was *so* tangled and messy that I couldn't even brush through it. I decided the only way I could possibly fix it was by cutting the tangles out. So I got a pair of scissors and started cutting away knots."

The audience gasped, then began laughing.

"I'm sure you can see where this is going," Luna said, laughing along with them. "You can only imagine; I looked dreadful! Luckily, it wasn't long after that I discovered Solar Glow. Their deep conditioner really helps keep my hair sleek and smooth. It's a miracle worker." She grinned, proud that she had figured out a way to slip a product endorsement into a true story. "I even use it on Adora's fur sometimes." Luna leaned backward and searched the wings of the stage for her small pink pet. "Adora, sweetheart, where are you? Come out here and show this nice host and all the lovely guests your pretty fur." Adora raced out of the wings.

While the studio audience cheered and whooped, Rhea, Athena, and Juno all breathed a sigh of relief that Luna was somehow managing to divert Tam's attention from their own childhood stories. Rhea, who had a very specific and well-known childhood—raised as an orphan before her royal blood was discovered and she was moved to the palace—could think of no stories that wouldn't give her away. Athena, who had been raised in a firm, strict household, had no "fun" stories of childhood. And

Juno preferred to keep her family and personal life—both of which she cherished and fiercely missed—as private as possible. She rarely even talked about her family or past on Junoia with the other princesses.

"Look at this little sweetheart!" Tam shrieked, calling Adora up onto his lap. "What a love!" Adora, who was never unkind to anyone, nuzzled into Tam's arms and instantly charmed him. "Now, this reminds me of something else I wanted to ask the band about. Tonight, while you were performing, it was impossible to miss your *pets* doing a little show of their own onstage. Was it my imagination, or were they . . . *beatboxing* with you?! Was that planned?"

Luna giggled, somehow making it seem like they hadn't been just as surprised as everyone else about their pets' newfound musical skills. The five little critters really had been beatboxing up onstage—which was both strange and wonderful, a shock to them all. "They're a talented group," Luna said, winking. "We're very proud of them."

Tam patted Adora and plopped her up on the surface of his news desk. "This has been absolutely wonderful," he said. "But unfortunately, we'll have to save the rest of the band's childhood stories for our next meeting. We need to take a short break. But when we come back—this week's *Dancing with the Empress* castoff will show us some moves to get your body shaking! Don't go anywhere."

Someone on set yelled "Cut," and Tam leaped up. "Wonderful, SPACEPOP. Absolutely wonderful. Thank you so much for being marvelous guests tonight. I'm so sorry you weren't able to meet the empress live and in person, but perhaps next time you visit me on set we can arrange for a meet-and-greet."

"Maybe so," Athena said coldly, not at all disappointed that they hadn't seen Geela herself while they were on set. "Thank you for having us."

The rest of the band echoed their thanks, shook hands with Tam (Juno and Athena), gave hugs (Hera), exchanged cheek-kisses (Luna), and high-fived (Rhea), before heading off set. As the girls wandered through the studio to pack up their things and make their way to the tour bus, a familiar voice called out to them from down a long hall. "Juno! Luna! SPACEPOP!!!"

Spinning around, the girls watched as Bradbury—the group's self-proclaimed "biggest fan"—raced toward them. The chubby alien's fluffy puff of hair bounced as he lumbered down the hall. Bradbury waved, then flicked a tiny lever on the side of his glasses (the glasses also served as video screens and cameras). "Hey, guys!"

"Hi, Bradbury," they called out. By now, the band had gotten used to Bradbury turning up in the most unusual places. The popular vlogger was well-known in the galaxy—and his popularity had grown by leaps and bounds after launching the SPACEPOP fan site and essentially introducing the band to the world. Bradbury seemed to have unlimited access to planets and sets and arenas that normal creatures would never get to step foot or tentacle on.

"I was hoping I could do a follow-up exposé for my vlog—ask a few of the questions Tam didn't have time for tonight?" Bradbury grinned at the girls, blushing when his eyes came to rest on Juno. As she had been all night, Juno was still scowling . . . but that didn't seem to change the way Bradbury felt about her. He was positively smitten with rough-and-tough Juno, though he would never have the guts to admit it aloud. The two of them came from very different planets. "I've dug up some pretty great stuff about you girls, and I want to verify everything before I reveal your dirty little secrets!"

"Oh," Rhea said, trying to come up with some excuse to say no. The girls were all exhausted from the show, and they desperately needed to get back to the ship to plan their next mission. They had already spent far too long avoiding unpleasant questions from Tam, so further questions from Bradbury sounded very unappealing. But if Bradbury had dug up dirt of some kind, they really needed to deal with it. "Um . . ."

Bradbury grinned. "Please?"

"For you, Bradbury," Luna began sweetly. She had proved once again tonight that she was an expert at dealing with fans and press. "Anything!" She winked at the other girls, then said, "But we're all about to collapse, we're so tired. Could we possibly ask you for a *huge* favor and postpone our conversation until tomorrow? I promise it will be better for everyone."

Bradbury looked crushed, but a second later he seemed to brighten. He spoke quickly, his words pouring out as he said, "Actually, tomorrow would be okay! But if it's tomorrow, I have a favor to ask you in return. I'm hosting this private party on my home planet—Pallomo—and it would mean so much to me if you would consider coming by to play a few songs. I wouldn't usually ask, but there are going to be a few big concert promoters there, so it's good exposure, and Pallomo is really close, so it's maybe on the way to wherever you're going next. If you say *no*, which I hope you don't, I can't promise that those secrets I found out about you won't be spilled to the world sooner than you might like . . ." He took a deep breath and trailed off.

"Pallomo?" Athena asked, trying to hide her enthusiasm. Pallomo was one of the planets the Resistance suspected of housing Geela's Dungeon of Dark Doom! The other four princesses seemed to realize this a few seconds after Athena did. Juno's face split into a smile for the first time all night. Attending Bradbury's party would be the perfect excuse to slip onto the planet and do a little exploring! "We would be honored."

"Really?" Bradbury screamed. "Yay! Yay, yay, yay, yay! I'll get a travel authorization over to Chamberlin just as soon as I can, okay? And I promise you, we'll have a great time!"

CHAPTER 6

"WHAT KINDS OF SECRETS DO YOU THINK Bradbury has dug up?" Rhea asked later that night while the girls were all relaxing before bed. She was stitching a new skirt that had some sort of strange plastic tubes sticking out all over the place.

"With Bradbury, you can never be sure." Juno looked up from her sketch pad. She had been working on new designs for the front of her bass drum, since she liked to make her kit look a little bit different for every performance. "I still don't totally trust the guy."

"He's harmless," Luna said, waving her off. She pulled a brush through her hair, glancing up every few seconds at a small holo-screen that was replaying all the day's vlog and blog uploads that included SPACEPOP. Luna kept close tabs on the band's social media presence and made sure they were always quick to respond to any kind of press that popped up. "I'm sure it's something silly, nothing to worry about."

Athena sat down at her keyboard and played a few notes, once again trying to work out the melody and lyrics for the new song they had been struggling with for days. "But what if it's not? What if he knows something about our *actual* pasts and is planning to reveal the truth to the galaxy? Tonight he said he was planning to blackmail us if we'd said no to playing at his party."

"Yeah," Hera said, looking up from her downward dog. "That was kind of weird. Blackmail isn't very nice."

Luna shrugged. "Look on the bright side. No matter how it all went down, we now have a free ticket to get onto Pallomo. We get to explore the second planet and search for our parents." She paused, her brush mid-stroke. "Oh my Grock! Hansome is going to be *so* excited. Can I be the one to tell him we're going to Pallomo tomorrow?"

"Fine." Rhea shrugged. "But you have to wait until morning, so he doesn't have time to swoop in and ride along again. He's much more of a liability than an asset."

"Agreed," said Athena. "But we certainly do need to

tell him before we go. I'm sure the Resistance will have some intelligence that will be useful to us in our search."

"We'd be fools to go in blind," agreed Juno. "And I'm *not* a fool."

Hera finished up her final sun salutation, muttered "Namaste" at no one in particular, and then said, "Speaking of smart, we all ought to get into bed now. We have a big day tomorrow, and proper rest is essential for keeping our wits about us."

Rhea snorted. She and Luna were both night owls, so it would be hours before either of them would be ready to curl up under their covers. Both of them were usually especially wired on performance nights. On the other hand, Hera, Athena, and Juno were all usually out early and up with the sun. It caused more than a few problems, considering the tight space on the bus. The walls weren't exactly soundproof. When they slipped out to go to the bathroom late at night, they could always hear Chamberlin snoring through the closed door to his bedroom.

"I don't think I can go to bed until I have at least a few lines of our new song down," said Athena. "I'm so worked up right now, and I want to use some of this energy to try to figure out *something*."

"I'll help you," Luna said, wrapping her hair up into a giant French twist. She pressed a pin into her mass of hair, then settled in next to the keyboard, closing her eyes as Athena tapped out a string of notes.

Suddenly, Luna began to sing. "When I am low . . ." Athena nodded, urging her to continue. Luna opened her eyes and smiled at Hera, then sang on. ". . . I know just who to call on."

"That's really pretty," Hera said, gently rubbing the soft fur under Roxie's ears. She pulled out her camera and snapped a few shots of Luna in action while Athena continued to tap out notes. Then Hera set her camera down and exclaimed, "How about something like this for the next line: Wherever I go, I know I got someone to count on."

Luna grinned, singing along as Hera picked up her instrument and layered on a bass line. The girls' collection of pets began to beatbox along, proving that what they had done on air during *The Geela Hour* hadn't been a fluke. "That's *so* cute," Luna said, clapping. "We should really make them a regular part of our shows. Our fans will go crazy!"

Luna, Athena, and Hera picked up where they had left off. Rhea strummed along, following Athena's lead on the keyboard. Juno tapped out a beat, waiting for her moment. After a few wordless minutes, Athena quietly sang out, "And I know I'll be all right, 'cause I got you by my side . . ." She looked up and flashed one of her rare smiles. "This sounds pretty good."

They had been working for nearly half an hour when Juno—who was still tapping on the rim of one of her drums—suddenly asked, "Do you really think we'll find our parents during one of these missions?"

Silence fell over the room. For a long moment, no one said anything. "Yeah," Luna finally whispered. "I do."

"What makes you think so?" Juno asked, her face stony as she tried to hold back her tears. "Is it just because you have so much faith in your beloved Captain Hansome?"

"It has nothing to do with my faith in Hansome," Luna said defiantly. She jutted out her chin and blurted, "I believe we'll find them because I have faith in us."

Again the room grew quiet. It was such a surprising sentiment, coming from Luna. For the first few weeks the princesses had spent together, Luna had been reluctant to consider herself a true member of the group. Even now, after they'd written a number of songs and begun to figure out how to coexist, she was usually so focused on what was best for *Luna* that it often seemed as if she was working toward an entirely different objective than the rest of them. But in that one simple statement, she had just solidified herself as one of the team.

"Luna's right. We will achieve our goal," Athena said

finally. "It's not a matter of if we will find our families and defeat Geela, but when."

"Maybe we'll even find them tomorrow," Hera said hopefully.

"Or maybe it *won't* be tomorrow," Rhea added. "Regardless, we're not giving up until we've found the Dungeon of Dark Doom and stopped Geela's reign of terror for good. We have no choice but to destroy her and take back our lives. None of us is stopping until we've done that. We're in this together."

Luna leaned against Juno's shoulder. The two girls—who had been raised worlds apart—rarely saw eye to eye. But that didn't mean they hadn't grown to care for each other. As much as they drove each other crazy, neither wanted to see the other girl suffering. "I know how much you're hurting," Luna murmured quietly. "Just know we're all doing everything we can to bring you back to them. We understand; we're all there with you."

Hera chimed in, "And I hope you know you can lean on us whenever you need someone to cry on, Juno."

Juno sniffled. She looked tough on the outside, but even the hardest shells developed cracks if they were hit hard enough. "Thanks, guys."

"Group hug?" Hera suggested hopefully.

This elicited a giant groan from all the other girls. But finally, reluctantly, Juno held out her arms. "Go on, then," she said. "Let me—" Before she finished speaking, Juno was knocked flat on her back as, one after another, each of the princesses' pets launched themselves at her like a bunch of furry missiles. Then the rest of the band joined the little critters, and soon everyone was laughing and crying together in a mess of arms and fur.

CHAPTER 7

NONE OF THE PRINCESSES HAD BEEN TO THE TINY plant of Pallomo before receiving the invitation to play at Bradbury's private party. During their sheltered royal lives, they had each been tucked away behind gates, fences, and sturdy stone walls, focused on things that were happening on their own planets and not much else. Of course, they all had been *invited* to visit other planets in the galaxy for royal business—but none of them had done much of that before Geela's takeover. Considering Pallomo was one of the smallest and least populated planets in the galaxy, it had certainly never warranted a visit from any of the royal families.

When their space bus landed, the first thing the girls noticed about Pallomo was just how much all the citizens of the planet looked like Bradbury. Nearly everyone—except the balding folk—had a similar fluffy tuft of hair, and the planet's entire population was exceedingly short and stocky. Even stooped-over Chamberlin appeared tall next to most of the Pallomo citizens. Unlike most planets in the galaxy, which were teeming with a wide variety of alien life, Pallomo was very homogeneous—all the inhabitants looked as if they could be related. It was obvious not many residents who had been born elsewhere had chosen to relocate to Pallomo to make a new life.

The second thing they all noticed was the overwhelming presence of Geela's Android Soldiers on the planet. The hulking metal beasts were discreetly stationed every ten feet or so, keeping a watchful eye on the seemingly peaceful residents who were going about their day. The planet's only city was bustling with activity but nearly silent. It was almost as if everyone walking to and fro was nervous to speak aloud lest one of the guards notice them.

"I haven't seen this many of those metal beasts in one place since Geela's army invaded Heralda," Hera said, shuddering. "Not something I'd been hoping to see again."

"It seems weird that she would assign so many of her troops to this tiny planet. Maybe their presence is a good sign she's hiding something important here," Athena noted.

"Like the Dungeon of Dark Doom," Hera agreed.

When the band received their travel authorization from Bradbury early that morning, their party host had told them to park the space bus right in front of Pallomo's main government building, where he would be waiting for them. No one had considered *why* they would be meeting Bradbury at the government building—but perhaps they should have.

As the band made their way across a wide metal bridge toward the building's arched entryway, every one of Geela's Android Soldiers kept a close watch on the group. The creatures' glowing metal eyes followed the girls' every movement, though their metal-clad bodies remained motionless. As soon as they reached the front doors, Chamberlin scanned the area and whispered, "Do any of you find it strange that this government building appears completely deserted, except for Geela's guards?"

Athena, too, looked around. She thought back to the conversation they'd had with Captain Hansome that morning, wherein the rebel leader shared everything the Resistance knew about the planet of Pallomo. "When we were discussing the mission, Hansome did say Geela has taken over the government building here on Pallomo. Perhaps she's fired the staff and no one works here anymore?"

"I highly doubt that," scoffed Juno. "That would mean *she* would have to figure out how to do the dull daily tasks necessary to keep the planet running. I'm certain she can't be bothered to figure out all those pesky little details."

"So where is everyone?" Hera asked. "Maybe it's siesta time?"

"I also doubt Geela would allow anyone time for a midday nap," Juno said.

"Walk carefully and do not stomp on a snoozing dragon . . ."

"What?" Rhea giggled. "Where did you get that saying, Chamberlin?"

"From the famous philosopher . . ." Chamberlin began. He muttered something that sounded like *Bluh-blug-blah.*

"Bluh-blug-blah?" Rhea echoed, an amused smile plastered across her face. "Who, exactly, is Bluh-blug-blah?"

"The wise philosopher who once said, 'Walk carefully and do not stomp on a snoozing dragon.'" Chamberlin cleared his throat. "I just think we ought to be careful, is all."

"Oh, Chamberlin," Luna sighed. "We abandoned caution long ago. If we're going to succeed in overthrowing Geela, we can't afford to be careful."

Chamberlin cleared his throat again—and then again. "Maybe *you* have abandoned caution, but I most certainly have not."

Ignoring Chamberlin's hesitation, the five girls—followed reluctantly by their "manager"—stepped into the expansive and run-down front hall of Pallomo's government building. As promised, Bradbury was standing in the center of the hall, waving to them. "Hi," he squeaked. Something about his voice was off, and the look on his face was far less jovial than it usually was when he came face-to-face with his favorite band. "I hope you, uh, had a nice trip here? The weather on Pallomo is lovely today, is it not?"

"It's great," Juno said, giving him a funny look. "Everything all good for your party?"

"About that . . ." Bradbury's voice cracked, and suddenly he turned very red. Thin rivulets of sweat rolled down his doughy face, and he started to blink quickly. "There's been a slight change of plans."

"What kind of change?" Athena asked, immediately on guard.

"Wonderful news all around!" interrupted an all-too-familiar voice. The band swiveled to face Geela, who swept forward from behind a pillar. "Instead of Bradbury's pitiful party of nobodies, tonight you'll be dining with *me*!"

CHAPTER 8

BRADBURY STARED HOPELESSLY AT SPACEPOP, looking as horrified as the band felt. Geela smirked at them all, her slippery smile as fake as the hair on her head. "I hope you're not too disappointed, but I've hijacked Bradbury's useless 'private party' and turned it into a lovely get-to-know-you for the five of you . . . and me!"

The so-called empress paused, letting the impact of this revelation sink in. "I've invited a few of my closest associates to join me at a special private event with the galaxy's hottest new musical act." She sneered, adding, "That's *you*, apparently. Since I missed the chance to chat with you on the set of *The Geela Hour* last night, I thought it would be a good thing for the six of us to spend some time getting to know each other a little better."

Rhea snuck a peek at Bradbury, whose eyes were now raining tears. No matter how much the poor creature had been brainwashed into admiring Geela, even he could see she was terrifying up close. It was unlikely that he would have arranged a private meet-and-greet between SPACEPOP and the so-called empress without asking the band first. Rhea was pretty certain their pal Bradbury had been forced to cancel his party and set up this bait-and-switch in its place. Instead of being furious, she felt bad for him.

"Well?" Geela prompted, after the band stared at her without saying anything. "Aren't you delighted?"

A low growl built up in Juno's throat. But before she could let it out, Luna cheerfully said, "Yes, so delighted. What a treat." She gave the others the briefest of looks that said, *Now is not the time to fight.*

"Then come," barked Geela. "All of you. The short, chubby pest and your old man, too." She spun around and led the band, Chamberlin, and Bradbury through a maze of corridors. Rand stumbled along after the group, his arms laden down with instruments and cords. The roadie looked positively stunned—he was a *huge* Geela fan and had probably never imagined he would have the opportunity to stand so close to a true legend.

While they walked, Athena remained at the back of the line—just behind Rand—subtly placing trackers every twenty feet or so. She wanted to ensure that they could find their way back to the entrance, if the need arose. She refused to trust Geela, even with good old Bradbury and his camera glasses around.

With a flourish, Geela ushered them into an enormous ballroom. The space was filled with expensive food (the first truly royal feast any of them had seen since fleeing their home planets), ice sculptures (all carved to look like Geela's head, though each wore a slightly different facial expression), and sumptuous chairs and banquettes scattered around the room.

Luna drew in a quick breath—she had been craving this sort of elegance for weeks. Platters heaped with caviar and desserts, elegant tiny bites paraded around by gorgeous, well-dressed waiters. Luna beamed at one of the most adorable waiters, who winked at her. She let her breath back out again.

"Remember whose party this is . . ." whispered Juno, nudging her. "Don't fraternize with the enemy."

"I know," snapped Luna. She gazed longingly at the fabulous treats and the bounty of even more fabulous guys. "I'm just looking—I promise not to touch."

There was a smattering of applause when the group entered the room. The party guests were made up of an odd assortment of Pallomo government workers, a collection of Geela's Android Soldiers, and an eclectic mix of aliens who—based on their name tags—were all employed by Geela and stood cowering in the corners of the room.

"Do you mind if I live-stream the party?" Bradbury asked, his voice shaking.

"Why not?" Geela said breezily. "My hair looks amazing today."

Bradbury flicked a few buttons on the side of his glasses, gazed slowly around the room, and then began speaking into the button on the cuff of his jacket. "Coming to you live from Pallomo . . ." he began in a low voice.

"Let the party begin!" Geela announced, waving her arm as though she was waiting for something dramatic to happen. Nothing did. For a long time, no one spoke. All the party guests just stared at SPACEPOP and Geela, who remained near the doors. "Isn't this marvelous?" Geela said after a long, awkward moment.

Rhea looked at her strangely. Though she had been to parties only in the palace on Rhealo, she was pretty sure most "parties" were usually a bit livelier than this. This was nothing but a collection of people who had obviously been forced to spend the evening in a room together. Based on the fact that everyone averted their eyes when she looked their way, it seemed that there was no one in attendance who would actually call Geela a friend.

For the briefest moment, both Rhea and Hera found themselves feeling sorry for the evil empress. Then they both remembered what she had done to the princesses' homes and families and how she mistreated the residents of their formerly peaceful galaxy—and any lingering pity was gone.

"You know," Geela said, her voice echoing in the nearly silent room. She snapped her fingers at one of the circling waiters. When he swooped in, she plucked a raw field onion off a tray, popping it into her mouth in a single bite. "I sing, too."

The band stared at her, trying to mask their hatred. They all knew this was neither the time nor the place for them to exact their revenge on the evil empress—but that didn't make it any easier to be in a room with her. And none of them, under any circumstances, wanted to make small talk with her.

"Did you hear what I said?" Geela said, now snapping in Athena's face. "I am a *singer*."

"I see," Athena said coolly.

"I'll perform with you at your next concert," Geela announced. "Imagine the delight on everyone's faces when I—the incredible Empress Geela—appear onstage to share my talents with amateur performers such as yourselves."

"You want to perform with us?" Luna asked in a strained voice.

"Want?" Geela laughed, as though the idea of her *wanting* anything was ridiculous. "No. But I will."

"Oh, that's okay," Luna said, plastering on a fake smile. "I'm sure you have much more important things to be doing than singing with us."

"Like ruining our galaxy . . ." Juno whispered so quietly only Hera could hear.

"Ah, yes," Geela said, smirking. "You mean important things like destroying the former royal planets of the Pentangle so I can rebuild them to my liking?" Chamberlin squeaked, but Geela didn't seem to hear. "Or torturing the useless Pentangle royalty inside their new home in my Dungeon of Dark Doom?" She popped a tiny fish into her mouth, chewed, and then added in a low voice, "Speaking of which, I owe my ridiculous royal guests a visit. It's been too long since they've had the honor of my company."

With wide, innocent eyes, Luna managed to ask, "Will you . . ." *Gulp.* ". . . be visiting the prisoners tonight?"

"Tonight?" Geela snapped. "Impossible. I'm here at this *fabulous* dinner with you."

Realizing Luna was fishing for clues as to the dungeon's whereabouts, Rhea somehow found her voice to speak, too. She pressed, "Perhaps you'll go to them after the party?"

"Considering the Dungeon of Dark Doom is on a different planet, that's highly unlikely." Geela rolled her eyes, not seeming to realize that she had just eliminated Pallomo from the list of possible planets that could be hiding the prisoners. She had inadvertently given the Resistance a very important clue that made this unpleasant evening *very* worth it!

Before Geela could say anything more, one of her assistants slipped into the ballroom and handed her boss an oversize handbag. "I thought this might be a good time to bring out your new accessory, Your Highness?" the assistant said, bowing low. "Perhaps the kid with the glasses could get some footage of you with it to make the acquisition worthwhile?"

"Wonderful," Geela said darkly, swinging the bag on her arm. She glanced at Bradbury and called out, "Yoo-hoo! Runty cameraman! Get a shot of this. I think some of your fans might like to know that SPACEPOP and I have matching accessories!" Geela opened the bag's zipper and peered inside. "Ugh, pets," she sneered. "Such a nuisance. Am I right?" She looked up at the band, waiting for one of them to agree with her.

Hera opened her mouth to reply, but before she could firmly disagree, a small, fuzzy head with pointed ears poked up and out of Geela's handbag. "Wh-wha—?" Hera stuttered. "What is that?"

"It's one of those kwub-kwubs that have become so fashionable," Geela said, rolling her eyes. "I've learned that if I don't keep the horrible thing locked up all day, it's constantly trying to climb on me and nuzzle. *Nuzzle!* Do I look like a nuzzler? Taking it in seemed like a good idea at the time, but I absolutely detest the thing. "

"At the time?" Hera asked.

"My team ordered it from some sort of ridiculous pet-adoption event last weekend. They picked the so-called 'cutest' creature and told me carrying it around would soften my image. "

Hera squinted at the kwub-kwub stuffed into the bag. The poor little beast peeked out at her, quaking with fear. Hera recognized the critter immediately: it was the very same kwub-kwub she had snuggled with at the celebrity pet-adoption event just days earlier! "But—" Hera began, her voice catching. "But kwub-kwubs need affection. Without enough cuddling, they get very restless and agitated. They can become highly depressed, and—"

"Did I ask for a lesson in pet care?" Geela snapped, cutting her off. "I am all-knowing. The last thing I need is a lecture on fur care from *you*. You can't even keep your curls from frizzing. Now. Shall we play?"

"With the kwub-kwub?" Hera asked hopefully.

"You really are rather dim," Geela said, throwing her a pitying look. "I mean, shall we play for my party guests, of course. Consider this your audition."

"Audition for what?" Juno asked.

"To be my backup band. I've been looking for the right musicians to back up my vocals, and it seems you five ought to be given the chance to try out."

"You want *us* to audition to be your backup band?" Luna asked, a note of horror in her voice. Luna sang backup to *no one*.

"I know this is a great honor," Geela said. "It's highly unusual to have a chance to perform with such greatness so early on in your careers. But you need not be nervous. Tonight is our first performance together, so I'll go easy on you. Bratwick," she said, getting in Bradbury's face. "Make sure you capture this moment for the fans. The universe is about to witness something *extraordinary*!"

Moments later, the band was ushered to the front of the room, where their gear was already squeezed into a corner of a stage. None of the princesses wanted to sing with Geela, but they didn't have much of a choice. To defy her would ensure certain punishment—or worse.

Geela adjusted her hair (prompting Luna and Rhea to exchange a knowing glance) and then tapped her fingernail on a microphone to call the partygoers' attention to the stage. "I hope you are all prepared for a real treat. Presenting Geela and the SPACEPOP!"

There was a smattering of applause as everyone in the crowd shared confused looks. But when Geela screamed into the mic, "Cheer, you lowly fools!" they all jumped up and down and whooped and clapped. Bradbury cheered louder than anyone. He rushed to the front of the stage so he would be able to live-stream the entire concert for his—and SPACEPOP's—legions of fans galaxy-wide.

Geela turned to the band and announced, "Since you don't know any of *my* brilliant songs, why don't I do you a favor and start with one of yours? I will kick things off with your awful little 'hit,' 'We 'Bout to Start Something Big.'" After a fast, uneven count, Geela launched into the song—and butchered it.

Her voice sounded like death itself.

Many people in the audience covered their ears to try to hide from the horrific sound. Hera's ears stung. Rhea couldn't keep herself from laughing at the craziness of the situation. Though they couldn't even hear their instruments, the band did their best to keep up with her frantic pace. Luna tried to sing more loudly to cover up Geela's vocals, but Geela just shoved her out of the way and unplugged Luna's microphone.

At the end of the song, the party guests tried to sound enthusiastic. Geela smirked, cooed "You're welcome," and then launched into another song. There was no doubt in anyone's mind that Geela was *not* a singer. But no one could say it, of course.

Then, a few songs into the concert, things got even uglier. Some nervy audience member began to quietly chant, "SPACEPOP, SPACEPOP, SPACEPOP"—and it didn't take long for the chant to catch on. At first, Geela couldn't hear the crowd over the sounds of her own screeching. But when she realized what the crowd was chanting, she freaked out. In a fit of fury, she wrapped her long fingers around Hera's and Luna's arms and began to drag them off the stage.

From the front of the stage, Bradbury yelled, "Hey! Where are you going?"

But Geela was so overcome with anger that she didn't seem to hear him. She just tightened her grip and pulled harder. Hera and Luna both flailed and scrambled, trying to escape Geela's deathly hold. Suddenly, Hera felt Geela's fingers release her. Hera looked down and saw the tiny kwub-kwub cub had sunk his razor-sharp teeth into Geela's arm!

By then, the rest of the band had figured out what was happening. Juno, Athena, and Rhea stopped playing. Luna screamed. The crowd stopped chanting, and Geela froze.

In the silence that followed, Bradbury called out, "Once again, this is Bradbury—reporting *live*, from a *very* special concert on Pallomo."

CHAPTER 9

"IF GEELA DISLIKED US BEFORE, SHE'S GOING TO *hate* us now," Luna said, as soon as the band was safe and sound and miles away from the party on Pallomo. She collapsed onto one of the sofas in the space bus's living room and turned on some music. When she recognized the song as one sung by Arion IV—SPACEPOP's biggest musical rival—Luna quickly flicked to a different channel.

"I think my ears are still burning," Rhea said, exploding in a fit of giggles as she plopped down beside Luna. "In all my life, I've never heard anything as brutal as Geela's singing voice. She sounded like a goat trapped in a field of hungry lions!"

"*Sqwaaaa!*" Juno sang out, doing her best impression of Geela's voice. "*BLAAAAT!*" She put a hand over her neck and cringed. "How does she even make that sound? It hurts my throat!"

"We have to go back," Hera said, staring forlornly out the window of the space bus as the soft Pallomo landscape faded into a speck in the distance. The moment the band had returned to the bus, Chamberlin made himself tea, then blasted onto the space highway with no clear destination set. He was so eager to get away from Geela, in fact, that he had almost left Rand behind on Pallomo. The band's poor roadie had been racing toward the bus with a huge armload of gear as Chamberlin started up the bus. He'd made it through the huge bus door just in the nick of time.

"Back to that party?" Athena asked. "Are you crazy? Do you have a death wish?"

"I need to rescue the kwub-kwub!" Hera said through tears. "Geela keeps the poor thing locked up in a handbag, and he looked absolutely terrified! How did she even pass the adoption screening?"

"You think Geela filled out an adoption-application form?" Rhea snorted. In a sarcastic voice, she continued, "Yes, that's right. The woman who stormed our homes, took the entire royal court as her prisoners, declared herself empress of the galaxy . . . I'm absolutely certain she went through the usual channels and filled out an application to adopt her perfect pet."

"But there's no way she would have passed the screening!" Hera said, outraged. "The pet-rescue center ensures that each adoptive family knows how to properly care for their new friend before they place them in the home. I made sure of it!"

"Hera," Rhea said in a gentle voice. "I was being sarcastic."

"Oh." Hera sniffled. She crossed her arms and said defiantly, "I *will* rescue that little sweetheart. It's inhumane to adopt a pet just because you think it will improve your image. Geela disgusts me. Even more than she did before."

"And here I would have thought spending an afternoon together at an extremely awkward party might have made the two of you become friends," muttered Rhea. "Guess I was wrong."

"I can't believe Bradbury set us up like that," Luna said.

"I don't think he set us up," Athena said. "I honestly think he was just as surprised by Geela taking over his party as we were. The poor guy was sweating and crying and looked absolutely terrified. I'm glad he was able to get out of there when we did."

Juno added, "Thank Grock he was there today. If

Bradbury hadn't been live-streaming the party, just think what Geela would have done to us when the crowd turned on her and chanted our names instead of hers." She grinned. "That was amazing."

"It *was* amazing," Rhea said. "Not as cool? Dragging Hera and Luna offstage. That did happen, right? Or was I imagining it?"

"It happened! She is *really* strong," Hera said, giggling. "Do you know why she let me go? The kwub-kwub stuck his head out of her handbag and bit her! That sweet little thing was trying to save me . . ." She broke off, sobbing again. "And we didn't do anything to repay the favor! He's still trapped, living a horrible life in Geela's custody!"

"You know what's even sadder than that?" Juno asked. "Neither of you was able to defend yourselves when you knew you were being threatened. You had to rely on a *kwub-kwub* cub and Bradbury's video glasses to save you from Geela. Just think of what might have happened if we had been somewhere alone with her. What if we get trapped on one of the planets we're exploring, and we need to fight our way out? It's clear we need to do some more training. Right now."

Luna whined, "I *hate* fight training."

"Too bad. You all need to toughen up. There won't always be a kwub-kwub around to protect you." Juno led the girls into their bedroom common room, so as to avoid any awkward encounters with Rand. Thankfully, their oblivious roadie hadn't yet figured out the girls' secret side job for the Resistance, and they all planned to keep it that way. "Now, let's go over some of the basics."

Athena plunked down in front of her keyboard, tapping out the notes to her song-in-progress while Juno spoke.

"First off, prevention is the smartest form of self-defense," Juno began. "It's important to always be aware of your surroundings. Stay alert; never put yourself in a foolish spot. If you can avoid a dangerous situation altogether, that's ideal."

"We're spies," Rhea said drily. "It's part of the job to put ourselves into dangerous situations."

"Yeah," Juno said. "I know. That's why we have to go through the next part. We probably won't be able to avoid confrontation forever, so let's talk about what you do if someone's coming at you." She gestured to her pet, Skitter. "C'm'ere, Skitter. Will you help me demonstrate?"

Skitter yawned and trotted over to Juno. Mousy little Skitter was the most timid of all the girls' pets—but when she got scared, nervous, or felt threatened, Skitter grew to ten times her usual size. The little trick had come in handy more than once during her and Juno's life together.

"I'm going to try to attack you, okay, pal?" Juno said, nodding at Skitter. "I want you to show everyone how to defend yourself. Got it?"

Skitter nodded shyly. Juno lunged at her, and Skitter immediately began to grow. She thrust out one of her arms and aimed her still-tiny fist at Juno's eye socket.

"Good!" Juno said, leaping backward. "The eyes are one of the most vulnerable parts of the body. That's a great spot to launch a counterattack." Without warning, she threw herself at Skitter again. Skitter grew even larger and rammed the heel of her paw into Juno's nose.

"Yow!" Juno said, holding her fist over her nose. She pulled it away, revealing a thin trickle of blood.

"You're hurt!" Hera shrieked, rushing toward her with a tissue. "You're bleeding!"

Skitter meeped apologetically and nuzzled against Juno's leg. Juno swiped the back of her hand across her face and wiped the blood away. "It's okay, just a little blood. And, Skitter, don't worry about it—I told you to defend yourself. The nose is a great target. I'm fine." She turned to the other girls. "But you know what? Skitter's too good at this. Any of you want to give it a shot and try to defend yourselves against my attack?"

"I will," Rhea said reluctantly, after no one else jumped at the chance. She stood up and braced herself, and Juno came at her. Rhea ducked and covered her head, then screamed.

Juno groaned. "Are you serious?"

"You're tough, Juno!" said Rhea, shrugging. "I didn't want to get hit. It's scary when you charge at me like that."

"I assure you, Geela and her Android Soldiers are tougher than I am. Ducking and screaming for help are *not* going to help you in that situation. This time, when I come after you, go for my neck or knees. Those are two of the other most vulnerable parts of someone's body."

Juno attacked again—and again—and again. Each of the girls took a turn trying to defend herself against Juno's attacks. Juno showed them how to use their elbows, knees, and heads—the hardest parts of their bodies—to inflict the most damage on their attacker. They were all sweating and panting when Chamberlin knocked at the door a while later.

"Yes?" Juno snapped.

"Pardon the interruption," he said. "Captain Hansome is hoping to speak with you. He would like a report on today's mission." He looked around the girls' common room, worriedly noticing how spent and exhausted each of the girls looked. "But if you girls need a rest after all the excitement of today, I can tell him to check in later.

In fact, I think I'll do just that. I don't believe a discussion with the Resistance leader is the best idea for the moment. I can make you all a nice cup of tea and read a bit of poetry!"

"Captain Hansome? Captain Hansome!" Luna jumped up and glanced at herself in the mirror. She swiped on a fresh coat of lipstick and fluffed her hair. "Of *course* we want to talk to him!"

"Anything to escape Juno's fight training," Rhea said, relieved to have a chance to catch her breath. The other girls hustled after Luna. They couldn't wait to tell the Resistance captain all about the surprise encounter with Geela—and figure out their next move.

As soon as they had finished their report on the day, Hansome said, "We need to act fast. It's important that we stop this monster now! If she's planning to visit the royal prisoners, then . . ." He trailed off, leaving the if-then unspoken.

"There are three more planets for us to search," Athena said, all business. "We've ruled out Kantal-ka and Pallomo. That leaves Lud, Tik-tik, and Pluton."

Chamberlin cleared his throat, but everyone ignored him.

"Indeed," Hansome said, rubbing his chin stubble thoughtfully. "How will we get you authorization to visit each of those planets as soon as possible?"

Again, Chamberlin cleared his throat. "Might I have a word?"

"What is it, Chamberlin?" Captain Hansome snapped.

"Moments before you called, I received a message from the Mighty Kra's manager. Their opening band has come down with a bug, and they're looking for someone to step in and take their place at a concert on Lud tomorrow night."

"Is now really the time to talk about show business?" Hansome said, irritated. "We are discussing much more important matters at the moment. Prioritize!"

Chamberlin cleared his throat. "The Mighty Kra have asked SPACEPOP to fill in as their opening act. On Lud."

"Wonderful," Hansome groaned. "Please, could you wait to discuss this namby-pamby band business later?"

Athena broke in, "What Chamberlin is trying to say is, this is a great opportunity to get the authorization we need to land on Lud!"

Hansome blinked rapidly. He was obviously embarrassed that he hadn't made the connection himself. He made his voice sound like a broken robot and said, "What's that? Sor-sorry. I think we-we-we have a bad connection! I don't think I heard you correctly, Chamberlin. Did you say something about Lud? What fantastic news. Go forth with care and caution, SPACEPOP. I'll send over everything the Resistance knows about Lud. We are all counting on you!" Before the princesses could say anything more, the hologram fizzled and went black.

"To Lud?" Athena asked, even though it was pretty clear what their marching orders were.

Chamberlin sighed and collapsed into the pilot's chair at the front of the bus. "To Lud."

CHAPTER 10

"THE MIGHTY KRA!" LUNA WHOOPED, JUMPING UP the moment the space bus landed on Lud late the next afternoon. "We are about to meet the Mighty Kra!" Adora hopped up and down beside her, unsure of what was so exciting—but thrilled to be part of the happy moment nonetheless.

"Hang on," Athena said, putting her hand on Luna's arm. Mykie copied her action, dropping a paw on Adora's furry back to settle her down, too. "Can we just figure out this next line? I'm afraid we'll lose our flow if we stop now." Athena plinked out a few notes on her keyboard, singing pieces of their new song. "When I am low, I know just who to call on. Wherever I go, I know I got someone to count on."

Luna layered on the next line: "And I know I'll be all right, 'cause I got you by my side . . ." She trailed off and then suddenly looked up, her face bright. She fanned her hands in the air and sang out, "So I know I'll never fall behind . . . 'cause you got my back for all of time."

"That's sounding really nice." Rhea glanced up from her sketch pad. She and Juno had both been drawing for hours—Rhea was working on a few new fashion designs to update the band's onstage looks; Juno was sketching a graphic novel retelling of the day they'd saved Captain Hansome and Chamberlin from the floating platform on Kantal-ka. Rhea tapped her sketching stylus on her bottom lip and said, "What if you added something like this: And you know this love is certified, 'cause I got you by my side."

Hera stepped out of her bedroom, her head caught in the neck of her show costume. In a muffled voice, she called out, "I think this is going to be an important song for SPACEPOP." She shimmied into her dress and zipped herself up. Unlike Athena, Hera was mostly dressed but hadn't yet put on any of her stage makeup. Hera preferred to go au naturel as long as possible. But even she had to admit that makeup helped the girls remain incognito—and everyone looked horribly washed out with no makeup onstage.

"If we ever figure out the rest of the lyrics." Athena stood up, scrubbing at her eyes. "I feel like every time we take a step forward and write another line, the end of the song creeps further and further away." She slipped into her performance outfit, then packed a small bag with her rebel-mission outfit and a few new spy gadgets she'd been working on. "Everyone, toss your rebel gear in here," she instructed, holding the bag open. "We might not have time to come back to the bus between the show and our search for the dungeon."

As soon as they had everything together and had given their gear to Rand, the girls and their pets stepped out of the bus and onto the stark, industrial planet of Lud. Though it was just after dusk, the planet was completely lit up. The center of the capital city was built tall, with sleek office towers, apartment buildings that were hundreds of stories high, and a twisting maze of skyways and passages that connected most of the buildings so residents of Lud didn't need to go down to the ground floor of one tower in order to get to another building.

"Their energy grid must be off the charts," Hera mused, a note of disapproval in her voice. "It wouldn't kill them to turn off a few lights in the city when they're not using them."

"The roof of every building on Lud is outfitted with a complex network of solar panels," Chamberlin told her. "They harvest the sun's energy during the day and don't require any additional source of power to keep things running at full strength until midnight. The energy efficiency programs on Lud are considered a model for the rest of the galaxy."

"Oh," Hera said, blushing a deeper shade of rose. "Well, that's good, then."

The band made their way through the stage door of the auditorium where that night's show would be held. Every single person walking around backstage was wearing black, making SPACEPOP look like a garish rainbow splashed across a dark and dreary storm-cloud sky. "What's with all the black?" Rhea whispered, her voice loud enough for only her bandmates to hear.

"It's the new dress code on Lud," Chamberlin whispered back. "Geela's rule. Any Lud resident caught wearing anything but black will be taken into custody. Yet another way Geela is exerting her control over the people of the galaxy."

"That's cruel!" Rhea gasped. "Lud was one of the most fashion-forward planets in the galaxy. Now it's so drab here!"

"Geela's done worse," Juno pointed out. Then she glanced down. "But I do feel a little overdressed . . ."

"Who wants to come with me to introduce ourselves to the Mighty Kra?" Luna asked, looking around for some sign of the five guys in the galaxy's most popular boy band. The Mighty Kra usually dressed in all-black costumes, so they wouldn't necessarily be that easy to spot in this particular crowd. "I hope they're as cute in person as they are on TV."

Chamberlin led the girls and their pets through the messy and chaotic backstage to their dressing room. Just before she stepped inside the cramped changing area that would be their home for the next few hours, Luna pointed to a door across the hall. "There's the Mighty Kra's dressing room . . . should we stop over and say hi?"

"Stop in to flirt, you mean?" Rhea asked.

"Maybe," Luna said, grinning. She flipped her hair over her shoulder and said, "Literally the only guys we've been around lately have been Chamberlin, Rand, and a fuzzy hologram of Captain Hansome. Seeing all the cute waiters at Geela's party made me realize how much I miss being surrounded by warm-blooded, just-the-right-age guys. The palace on Lunaria was filled with hotties, and I'm going through serious withdrawal."

"Aren't the guys in the Mighty Kra of Hantalian descent? That's a cold-blooded race," Juno noted.

"Whatever," Luna said. "They're cute, talented, and

single. That's all that matters." She strode across the hall and knocked confidently on the boys' dressing room door. A tall, orange-skinned alien answered the door. His tan hair was slicked back, revealing sculpted cheekbones and a long, elegant neck. "Mack?" Luna said in a breathless voice. "I'm Luna—lead singer of SPACEPOP."

"Hey," Mack said, blinking slowly. He cocked his head and announced, "You look different in person."

"Oh," Luna said, laughing. "Better, I hope?"

"I guess," Mack said in a thick, soupy sort of voice. "Yeah, sure."

Luna studied him closely. Of all the guys in the Mighty Kra, Mack had never been her favorite. He wasn't as cute as Dane, the drummer. He didn't seem as nice as Dane, either. And now that she'd met him in person, she couldn't help thinking Mack looked and sounded much *worse* up close than he did in all the glossy photos and videos online. He always seemed pretty upbeat and interesting in interviews, but in person he looked sort of vacant. Like there wasn't much going on beneath his shiny exterior. But Luna chalked it up to preshow jitters and decided not to make a snap judgment—for once. "I just wanted to introduce myself before the show," she said, peering around Mack to wave to the rest of the band. She furrowed her brow. None of them even looked up from their mirrors to say hello. They were all doing their hair or applying a thick cream to their faces. The band's guitar player, Funt, was making strange smiling faces at himself in the mirror. "So, um, hey!"

"Hey," the rest of the Mighty Kra echoed without any enthusiasm. Luna waved again, then swished her hair around her shoulders, hoping to catch their attention. Still nothing.

"Well, if any of you guys want to hang out after the show or anything . . ." Luna began hopefully. After reading through Captain Hansome's mission documents, SPACEPOP had decided to wait until after midnight that night to embark on their search for the Dungeon of Dark Doom. The Resistance had discovered that the planet's security systems and lighting grid went into sleep mode after midnight to conserve energy. So the rebels would be least likely to be caught on their search mission if they set out after things shut down for the night. Luna went on, "Grab a bite to eat, maybe just hang out and listen to music . . ." Luna couldn't help but wonder: Would Captain Hansome feel jealous if she was spotted on a date with another guy?

Mack shrugged. "I dunno."

"I bet the paparazzi would have a field day if they saw some of you out with some of us," Luna said, winking.

"Paparazzi?" Dane said, suddenly looking away from

his mirror to study Luna. "If there are cameras there, I'm in."

Luna frowned. "I can't *guarantee* the paps will find us, but I'm sure we can figure out a way to get them to notice us."

"I'll consider it," Dane said, shrugging.

"Oh-*kay*," Luna said haughtily. She wasn't going to *beg* any of the Mighty Kra to go out with her! It was their loss if they didn't want to hang out. But she couldn't help feeling the slightest bit miffed—between Captain Hansome's obliviousness and a cold reaction to her from this boy band, she was feeling very unwanted lately! "Well, if any of you guys do want to hang out, you know where to find me. Um, us." She spun around and returned to her dressing room with the rest of the band.

"That went well," Rhea said drily. "Seems like you and the Mighty Kra have a very promising future ahead of you. Love at first sight."

Luna glared at her. "I'm sure I just caught them at a bad time."

"Uh-huh," Rhea said, laughing. "Wanna bet on it?"

"On what?" Luna snapped.

"If you end up hanging out with the Mighty Kra later, I'll make your bed for a week. And what the heck, if you win, I'll clean your room, too." Rhea thrust out her hand, waiting for Luna to shake.

"And if I don't?" Luna asked.

"If you don't, *you* make *my* bed for a week." Rhea cocked an eyebrow. "Deal?"

"We are on." Luna grinned. She had *never* lost a bet in her life, and she had no plans to start now.

"So, Dane, do you like being on the road most of the year?" Luna smiled sweetly across the table of an old-fashioned diner at Dane, the drummer from the Mighty Kra.

"S'okay," Dane muttered. He picked at his plate of salad, gazing forlornly out the window. He was obviously waiting for more cameras to show up. Every time a crew of paparazzi appeared outside the window of the diner, Dane came to life. But when there were no cameras, it was a very different story.

Even though their date was going absolutely terribly, Luna didn't seem to notice or care—she had won her bet with Rhea, she was on a date with one of the hottest singing sensations in the galaxy, *and* she now had a servant to make her bed and clean her room for a week. A week of luxury made an evening of Dane's horrible conversation almost worth it.

Juno—who had been suckered into accompanying

Luna on her date and was getting *nothing* out of the evening—disagreed. She had never met anyone as boring and self-absorbed as Dane, and she couldn't believe Luna seemed totally oblivious to his lack of charm. Chamberlin owed her *big-time* for going along with Luna. Juno was still convinced Luna would have been just fine on her own, but their butler had insisted that someone go along, just in case. Just in case of *what* hadn't been clear. But since Juno was the most capable of brawling with a paparazzo, Chamberlin had begged her to be the third wheel.

Luna took a sip of her fizz-fizz. Dane glanced across the table at her. "Is that good?" He pushed dry river seaweed around on his own plate.

"Yeah," Luna said. "You should order one."

Dane laughed humorlessly. "Hardly. I don't eat—or drink—sweets."

"At all?" Luna asked, horrified. She and Juno exchanged a look.

"I don't want to mess up my skin." Dane ran his fingers across his unblemished cheek, then pulled a small mirror out of his pocket and smiled at his reflection.

"A fizz-fizz from time to time isn't going to do much damage."

"I disagree," Dane said curtly.

For a long time, they all sat there quietly, not saying

anything. Luna gazed lovingly at Dane while she slurped down her treat. Meanwhile, Dane stared lovingly into his reflection in the napkin holder. Juno thought about how she would rather be doing yoga with Hera—and that was saying a lot.

The silence stretched on. Luna tried to make conversation about music, but Dane seemed interested only in talking about songs by the Mighty Kra. Luna attempted to ask Dane more questions about life on the road and if he had any pets or hobbies, which made Dane go on and on about the amazing speeder he'd had custom-painted to match his skin. Eager to find *something* they connected on that would make Dane talk about anything other than himself, Luna brought up books. Dane lit up—and began reading the girls passages from the soon-to-be-published authorized biography of the Mighty Kra.

For the first time in her life, Luna had run out of things to say. And her drink was almost gone. "Juno, can you join me in the restroom for a sec?" she said cheerfully as Dane put his e-reader away.

"Gladly," Juno grunted, sliding out of her seat. When they got to the bathroom, Juno put her hands on her hips and glared at Luna. "This is torture," she said, preparing for a fight.

But instead of fighting back, Luna surprised Juno by exploding in a fit of giggles. "He's *awful!*"

"Really?" Juno said, surprised. "You noticed?"

"I'm not blind, Juno. He's completely self-absorbed. Being totally gorgeous does not make up for being a majorly egotistical dud." She grinned at herself in the mirror. "I should know—I have looks *and* personality. I've learned from experience that you can totally have both."

Juno shook her head. "You're a piece of work, Luna."

"At least *I* am an *interesting* piece of work," Luna said. "Dane is like a cheap cardboard cutout of a piece of work. Want to get out of here?"

"Like, just leave?" Juno narrowed her eyes. A hint of a smile crossed her lips. Maybe she had underestimated Luna's ability to judge people after all. "Without saying goodbye?"

"Serves him right," Luna said. She tipped her head in the direction of the bathroom window and giggled. "Shall we put some of our spy skills to good use and take the back way out?" Then she scrambled up onto the bathroom counter and opened the window, glancing back over her shoulder to ask, "How long do you think it will take good old Dane to realize we're gone?"

CHAPTER 11

BY THE TIME LUNA AND JUNO GOT BACK TO THE band's dressing room, the other three girls were ready and waiting in their all-black rebel costumes . . . and they did *not* look happy. In fairness, Juno and Luna had returned from their date much later than they had promised to—but there was a good reason for their tardiness, and they were returning with some very good news.

"Sorry we're late," Luna said breathlessly. "But we brought everyone doughnuts to make up for it! Who wants a tasty treat before tonight's mission?"

"Me!" Hera cheered, reaching for one of the glazed raised doughnuts in a plain white box. All five of the girls' pets clustered around her, grabbing at the snacks with their furry paws. There was a brief tussle between Roxie and Springle, but things were quickly resolved when the doughnut they'd been fighting over ripped in half.

Athena and Rhea stared impassively at the doughnuts, unwilling to be so easily won over. "What took you so long? You promised you'd be back before midnight," Athena scolded. "It's exactly quarter after, which means we've lost fifteen minutes of our search time."

"I'm really sorry," Luna said. "But we're here now. And we come bearing snacks and news!"

"You missed a visit from Bradbury," Rhea grumped. "You can imagine his disappointment when he had to interview his three *least* favorite members of SPACEPOP— he clearly likes both of you more than he likes the rest of us put together. He spent most of our interview time blubbering about Geela's party and how glamorous it was, and then he wouldn't stop talking about the secret he can't wait to reveal to the world. He wouldn't tell us what it was without Luna in the room." She glared at both Luna and Juno. "And you obviously weren't here."

"Luna said we're sorry," Juno snapped. "Do you want to hear about our night, or no?"

Athena nodded coolly, so Juno began the story. She breezed over the details of their so-called date with Dane, starting the story with their escape out the bathroom window. After the two girls snuck out of the diner, they quickly realized they were seriously turned around and apparently lost on the deserted streets of Lud.

"We raced around for a while," Juno told the others as she slipped into her rebel gear. "But it was really hard to get a bearing on where we were, considering we were surrounded on all sides by tall industrial towers and glowing billboards. It felt like being inside a huge metal maze. The whole thing brought back crazy memories of my experience on *Fight or Flight*."

Luna jumped in and continued their story. "So we're walking down this long block when, all of a sudden, one of Geela's Android Soldiers came zooming toward us. In this awful, tinny voice, it screamed, 'You are under arrest for dress code violation! I'm taking you in.' I was totally getting ready to fight back and run when Juno said—"

"Let him take us," Juno said, cutting her off to continue the story.

"What?!" Chamberlin gasped. Their butler, who had appeared to be dozing in a corner of the dressing room when the girls returned from their outing, was now up and alert. "Why would you let one of those beasts take you? Juno, I sent you along with Luna to protect her, not to let her be taken into custody!"

Juno laughed. "Yeah, yeah, I know. Here's the thing: it

was one stupid metal droid, arresting us for a dress code violation. I knew I could take him down if I needed to. But by going along with him, I hoped the awful Android Soldier would lead us straight to Geela's headquarters here on Lud—thus simplifying our search for the Dungeon of Dark Doom later tonight."

"You *let* yourselves get arrested so you could find out where Geela takes prisoners?" Athena blurted out. "That was incredibly risky . . . and extremely brilliant."

"Thank you!" Luna said cheerfully.

"So we let him take us in for the minor dress code infraction," Juno went on. "But before he could get the paperwork under way, we stunned him and the rest of the desk guards using Athena's hypno-glasses."

"You got to use the hypno-glasses?" Hera asked, pouting. "Lucky duck!"

"I hid them in my bag before Luna and I went out with Dane tonight," Juno explained. "Figured I could use them on Luna *or* Dane if I'd had enough chaperone time and needed to make their date end."

"Our *spy* gadgets are supposed to be reserved for spy missions," Athena scolded.

"Then it's a good thing I had them, eh?" Juno said. "Since we were doing some spying? It got us out of Geela's custody before they had time to take our mug shots *or* book us. No one will ever know we were there."

"Dane was a dud, but two good things came of our date tonight," Luna said proudly. "We now know where Geela's administrative headquarters are here on Lud . . . *and* we stole some of her doughnuts before we escaped. Win-win!"

"Win-win," Rhea echoed, holding her doughnut in the air. The other girls all grabbed a doughnut as Rhea went on, "To being arrested for dressing well, stealing the empress's doughnuts, and getting us off to a very fortu-itous start on tonight's reconnaissance mission. Cheers!"

Less than an hour later, the five spies were standing at the base of Geela's administrative building on Lud— ready to continue the search for their parents. Unlike all the other buildings on the planet of Lud, Geela's administrative building was short and stocky. Towering only two stories high, it would be easy to miss it com-pletely, surrounded as it was by all the tall, magnificent towers.

"Follow me," Athena said. She shot a length of rope out of her belt, tugged it to be sure it had hooked to the side of the roof, and then climbed up the side of the building. The others quickly followed. A few minutes later, the five spies were stepping carefully among hundreds of solar panels on the roof of the building. "I have to admit, I'm glad Chamberlin sat this one out," Athena said quietly.

The girls' nervous butler usually insisted that he accompany the princesses on their rebel missions. But as the assignments had grown more and more difficult, he had begun to opt out of their adventures more often.

"The guy can make a mean cup of tea," Rhea said. "But I'm not sure he's cut out for climbing a rope up the side of a building. Or, you know, climbing out of his chair after nine o'clock."

The girls walked silently around the solar panels, and eventually they arrived at an air shaft in the center of the roof. "Entry point," Juno said, pointing. Carefully and quietly, the girls slipped into the air shaft and snuck into the top floor of the building. Inside, everything was very dark, and the girls paused a moment to let their eyes adjust to the blackness. But after only a moment, they noticed there was a very faint glow coming from tiny lights spaced out every ten feet or so in the floors. The track lighting wasn't bright, but the faint glimmer of yellow certainly would help.

After a brief exploration of the top floor, they discovered that Geela's administrative building was—as the Resistance had suspected—*much* larger than it seemed from the outside. While there were only two stories of offices and such aboveground—both of which were devoid of staff at such a late hour—the tower stretched 111 stories belowground. Someone had posted a handy guide to floors beside the elevator shaft. The floors nearest ground level were marked with boring labels such as "Offices," "Administration," and "Personnel." The bottom ten floors, however, were labeled "Restricted."

"Seems like a few hundred feet belowground, on a restricted floor, would be a mighty fine place to hide something called the Dungeon of Dark Doom," Luna said quietly.

"Very true," agreed Athena.

"We should focus our search at the bottom of the building, yeah?" Juno said. The others quickly agreed. But when they pressed the button in the elevator to go down, nothing happened.

"No power to make the elevator run!" Hera whispered. "Not until morning, remember?"

"Right," said Athena.

"A little exercise won't kill us," said Juno, leading them toward the stairs.

"Speak for yourself," Luna grumbled. She was huffing and puffing two flights of stairs into the journey, and her hair began to droop.

It took much longer than any of them would have expected to climb one hundred stories down. When they finally reached the bottommost floors of the building, it then took nearly half an hour for them to come up with a strategy to avoid the cadre of patrols roaming the heavily guarded corridors. They sent a small bug droid in ahead of them to take footage of the guards' actions for a while. By studying the footage carefully, they were able to figure out the guards' rotation schedule—and determine when the coast would be clear. If they timed their actions carefully, they might avoid being seen.

When it was go time, the girls split up into two groups so they could search as much of the restricted area as possible before daybreak. By splitting up into smaller groups, they were also much less likely to attract notice. Hera was thrilled, since dividing and conquering meant she would get to use her lipstick communicator—finally!—to report any findings back to the other team.

But sadly, after a long and stressful search, there was nothing interesting to report.

"Nine of ten floors searched, and still no sign that the Dungeon of Dark Doom is hidden here on Lud," Athena said quietly. The team had reconvened in the stairwell right outside the bottommost floor of the building. There was only one floor left to search, and everyone was losing hope.

"There are still two more planets to explore," Rhea said in an upbeat voice. "If the dungeon isn't here on Lud, all hope is not lost."

"Yeah." Juno nodded. "I just want to find them soon, you know? After hearing Geela talk about torturing my family, it's hard to be patient."

"We'll find them," Luna promised, knowing full well there were no guarantees when it came to Geela. But she had no choice but to promise and then *make* the promise come true. "We will."

The bottom floor of Geela's central command center on Lud was extremely different from everywhere else they had searched in the past weeks. The floors of the basement level were covered in lush carpet, rather than the cheap marble or polished concrete Geela used in many of her other buildings. The walls were covered in soft tapestries and paintings. Even in the dim light, it was clear that this floor was Geela's lair on Lud. It was also clear that this was most definitely not the Dungeon of Dark Doom.

Still, the girls searched for any sign of strange doors or secret passageways, anything that might lead them to a hidden torture chamber. But the only things they found were rooms stuffed with crazy collections of things: one was wall-to-wall shoes (everything from last-century clogs to elegant, sky-high stilettos), another had an assortment of yoga pants and sweats mixed together with stolen designs from the season finale of *Galactic Fashion*, and a third was filled with *dozens* of wigs, each styled in an elegant hairstyle.

"You know what we've gotta do . . ." Rhea said, grinning back at the others. "Obviously, Geela has an absurdly large collection of wigs. Surely she won't notice if a few go missing? We didn't find the prisoners, but I can assure you I'm not walking out of here empty-handed." She began to grab handfuls of wigs off the walls, stuffing them carelessly into her backpack. Juno, Athena, and Hera followed suit. They filled their bags as full as they possibly could, but still there were more.

"Wait! Wait!" Luna giggled. "I have an idea! We don't have to take them all. I have a couple bottles of Solar Glow hair spray with me. We can douse the wig hair with Solar Glow—I guarantee that if the product soaks into the hair for a couple hours, the wigs will fall apart. Don't tell the galaxy I said so, but Solar Glow destroys hair."

"Do you ever feel at *all* guilty that you're the one telling people to buy this stuff, even when you know it's awful?" Rhea asked, her eyebrows raised.

Luna shrugged and said, "Does anyone actually believe the stuff they tell you in commercials?" She handed Hera and Rhea bottles of hair spray, and they went to work covering every last wig with as much of the product as possible.

The girls were still laughing and celebrating when Athena called out, "I found something!" Masked behind one of the racks of wigs was a small door. The door wasn't locked, but Geela had obviously taken extra steps to keep the entrance to this room hidden. The girls crouched low and stepped inside. Their smiles slipped off their faces when they got a look at the space.

The hidden room was cozy and luxurious, filled with comfortable sofas and elegant display cases. It looked like the kind of living room a museum curator might have in her house. The walls were filled with extravagant art and shelves that displayed a huge collection of artifacts—treasures that Geela's troops had clearly harvested from the five princesses' former homes.

"This is the painting that was hanging in our castle's front hall on Heralda!" Hera shrieked.

The other girls shushed her. No matter how upset they all felt, this would be a terrible time to get caught. Lowering her voice, Hera said, "This painting has been in my family for centuries. She *stole* it. My great-great-great-great-grandfather painted it for our home when it was first built. It belongs on Heralda—not here, in Geela's creepy treasure room on Lud!"

"And this," Juno said, running her fingers across a chunk of hard stone. The stone was being used as a coaster for a half-full cup of juice in the center of a coffee table. Juno set the cup on the table, then flipped the stone over, revealing a child's handprint. "This must have been taken from the front hallway in the Junoia palace. This is my father's handprint, hidden inside the floor of our great hall when he was still a boy."

Each of the girls took a moment to look around at the shards of their old lives, now collected in messy piles in Geela's treasure room. "We must go," Athena said after a few minutes of reminiscing, her usually calm voice breaking.

"What is this?" Rhea asked, pointing to a tiny, jewel-encrusted box that was hanging from the center of the room in a glass case. It was clearly the showpiece of the room, visible from every seat and corner. "Which of our planets did this come from?"

No one answered.

"Does anyone recognize it?" Luna asked. "It's beautiful. It's not jewelry." She stepped closer to the glass case. "It almost looks like it's glowing."

"Could—" Rhea began. "Could it be Geela's? Perhaps this is an artifact from her own life?"

"Something of her father's, perhaps?" Athena wondered aloud. "I know, from listening to my parents talk about her, that Geela and her father were very close."

"It's ours now," Juno said, reaching toward the glass cylinder to remove the jewel-encrusted box from its spot. "My guess is, this either belonged to the royal family on one of our planets to begin with . . . or it's something that holds sentimental value for Geela."

Hera nodded. "Whichever it is, after all the damage she's done to our planets and people, she doesn't deserve to possess it anymore."

"I think we can all agree on that," Athena said curtly. "Take it and let's go. It will be light soon, so we can afford no further delays. We will have to figure out its importance later."

As they began their long, slow climb back up to the ground floor, the girls were quiet, tired, and lost in their thoughts.

To try to keep their spirits up, Rhea pulled one of Geela's long, curly-haired wigs out of her bag. She waved it in the air, dropped it on her head, and said, "Anyone else think it will be fun to see how cute Chamberlin looks in curls?" Their laughter made the last part of the climb just a little bit easier.

CHAPTER 12

"TONIGHT, ON *DANCING WITH THE EMPRESS*, WE'LL be doing the cha—" Tont, the slimy-skinned host of *Dancing with the Empress*, broke off midsentence and gaped at something offscreen. Luna looked up from doing her nails and watched the life-size hologram in the center of the space bus living room curiously. Luna was the only one of the princesses who could stand to watch Geela's shows. She didn't enjoy watching a life-size version of Geela strut around the living room, but Luna was convinced the awful woman might accidentally slip up and reveal a hint about the Dungeon of Dark Doom location while she was on-air. So Luna watched new episodes of *Dancing with the Empress*, Geela's design shows, *Cooking with G!*, and *The Empress* fairly religiously.

Luna continued to stare at the hologram in the center of the space bus living room, waiting to see why Tont was acting so strangely. There was no sound coming from the hologram, but Tont's face was moving just enough that Luna was pretty sure the video playback hadn't gotten frozen or anything. He just looked stunned into silence.

A moment later, Geela—dressed in an elaborate ball gown—stepped across the stage and joined her host in front of the main camera. The *Dancing with the Empress* host continued to stare, saying nothing. Finally, Geela snapped, "What is it, Tont?"

"She's wearing a turban!" Luna shrieked, calling the other girls into the room. "Look!"

In fact, Geela's head was wrapped tight in a paisley turban. "Even magnificent, all-powerful empresses have bad hair days from time to time," Geela snapped, refusing to look at the camera.

"Aw, poor thing. She should have tried Solar Glow. *Bad hair days begone!*" Luna said, repeating the product's advertising catchphrase.

"Maybe it wasn't such a good idea to leave your wigs unattended, G," Rhea said in a pitying voice. "Something bad could've happen to them."

Rand strolled into the room just as Rhea said that. He

glanced at the hologram of his beloved empress and shook his head. Rand *loved* Geela. In fact, most of his T-shirts had her face silk-screened across his ample belly. "Oh, man," Rand said sadly. "Her hair always looks so pretty. Why is she wearing that colorful toilet paper around her head?"

"It's a turban," Hera told him.

"Whatever it is, I liked the way she looked before," Rand pouted. Sighing and muttering to himself, he carried on through the living room to pour himself a bowl of Asteroid Crunch from the ship's kitchen. Just as he went out one door, the five SPACEPOP pets bounded in another—each wearing one of Geela's wigs. The five little critters looked utterly ridiculous in the too large, elaborate hairstyles. When they began to beatbox and dance around the room, it was impossible not to laugh.

But after watching a few seconds of their performance, Juno got serious again. Sarcastically, she said, "So we ruined the mighty empress's wigs and stole a few others. Major victory for the Resistance. Yay us!"

Athena nodded. "In the grand scheme of things, no, it's not a major victory—you're right. But it's a minor setback, and with enough minor setbacks, Geela will weaken. We're slowly breaking her down."

"We don't have time for slowly breaking her down," Juno said, punching the hologram. Her hand went right through Geela's arm. "She has our families. I want to shatter her empire, once and for all."

"We all do," Athena agreed. "So let's figure out a way to get clearance to land on the last two suspicious planets. Now that we've ruled out Kantal-ka, Lud, and Pallomo as hiding places for the Dungeon of Dark Doom, it is very likely Geela is hiding her prisoners—our families—on either Tik-tik or Pluton."

Luna took a deep breath and said, "I found a way to get to Tik-tik."

"Great!" Hera said. "A small gig or an arena thing?"

"Well . . ." Luna began. "There's this huge concert happening tomorrow night—it will be live-broadcast to the entire galaxy—and I got an invite."

"You did?" Athena asked, confused. "Why didn't the booking come through Chamberlin?"

"It's not a band thing," Luna told the others, biting her lip. "They only want me."

"You?" Juno asked.

"Me. I got an e-mail from the organizers this morning, asking if I wanted to be a part of it. They're calling the event *Sopranos Unplugged*, and some of the best-known soloists will be performing onstage together."

"You're not a solo artist," Athena reminded her. "You're part of a group. Our group."

"Yeah, about that . . . for this event, *unplugged* doesn't mean unplugged from our amps and mics and stuff—they want to see us unplugged from our backup bands. They're hoping to showcase the true artistry of solo voices."

Juno and Rhea gawked at Luna. "Your words or theirs?" Juno asked.

"Theirs," Luna said hurriedly. "I love playing with you guys, and I obviously asked if you could perform with me. But they said no. At this event, it's all about my voice." She swept her arms into the air and announced, "Luna . . . Live!" Then she hastily added, "Of course, I told them I needed SPACEPOP to come with me for backstage support, and, um, for wardrobe."

"As annoying as this is going to be, it is a way for us to get clearance to land on Tik-tik," said Rhea, cringing. "So *Luna Live*, here we come."

"Luna, you're on in five!" A production assistant popped her head inside Luna's dressing room. "Ready?"

"Almost," Luna said, spritzing her hair with one more blast of hair spray. She glanced at her bandmates, who were happily devouring all the snacks that had been delivered to Luna's dressing room. Luna chewed her lower lip nervously. "How do I look?"

"Okay," Rhea said thoughtfully, stepping forward. "But something's not quite right. You know what would look even better?"

Luna's eyes went wide. "What? What's wrong?"

Rhea reached out one hand and touched Luna's hair. "This." She pulled one of Geela's wigs out from behind her back and tried to stuff it over Luna's hair.

Luna batted it away. "Ew! Get that away from me."

"You look great," Rhea promised, giving her a quick hug. "Break a leg out there, okay? Make us all look good."

"I will," Luna promised. She took a deep breath. "I never thought I'd say this, but it's going to feel strange being up onstage without all of you behind me. I'm a little nervous."

"Don't be," Athena said. "You'll be great."

Luna smiled. "Thanks, Athena. Oh! And I hope you don't mind, but I borrowed the Amp It Up. I've been dying to see if that little box actually works as well as the company says it will. If it does, I'll certainly stand out on stage!" Athena started to say something, but Luna cut her off. "And since *you* totally object to it—I figure I can give it a shot on my own and see if it's worth using at one of our bigger shows. Fair enough?

Seems silly not to at least *try* the thing. It could be magic."

Athena shook her head, disapproving. "Just be careful. The letter they sent with it said if you use the amp wrong, glass can break and metal will shred. Seems unlikely such a tiny thing could do much damage, but be careful."

"I'm a pro," Luna said, smiling. "Amp me up, babe!" As she made her way to the stage for her turn in the solo spotlight, the other girls donned their Resistance outfits and prepared for their secret mission to find the Dungeon of Dark Doom.

Hansome had sent each of them a frost-proof under-layer that he promised would combat the subzero temperatures on Tik-tik. He had also sent along special breathing devices that would (hopefully) block out the horrible odor on the gaseous planet. Even Rand—who rarely complained about anything—had moaned about the stench on Tik-tik when they landed. Despite the frozen air, the atmosphere around the planet smelled like cooked brussels sprouts and swamp water. Chamberlin said it hadn't always smelled funny, but that everything about the Tik-tik air had changed since Geela's troops moved in.

"You know what seems a little odd?" Hera asked as they crept out the back of the theater into the frozen Tik-tik afternoon. Though the early-evening sky was bright and sunny, it was bitterly cold, and the girls' frosty breath clouded the air whenever they spoke. "It seems like this is the kind of show *Geela* would weasel her way into."

"Oh my Grock, you're right," Juno said, quickly putting her foot in the door before it closed and locked behind them. "If this is a showcase of the galaxy's most distinguished singers—broadcast live on one of the many networks Geela has taken control of—it seems like exactly the kind of thing she would have insisted she be included in."

"The mighty empress always gets her way," Rhea said. "So where is she?"

"It concerns me that she's not here," Athena said. "I don't think we should leave Luna alone in the theater until we're sure it's safe. I wouldn't put it past Geela to do something horrible that would eliminate the competition. If she wants to be a famous singer, the only way she's going to succeed is if there is literally *no* other music available in the galaxy."

The group raced back inside, quickly covering their Resistance outfits with a collection of fake furs and velvet capes they found on a stray wardrobe rack. They peered around a curtain to get a look at the performance that was taking place onstage. Luna and one of the other sopranos—Callista from Arion IV—were sitting on stools in the center of the stage, singing over each other. Floating camera bots surrounded the two of them while the small studio audience gazed up at them, rapt. Luna and Callista layered their vocals, their voices lifting and curling to fill the space.

"Luna sounds good," Juno said.

"She really does," said Rhea. "Her diva attitude drives me crazy ninety percent of the time, but we're definitely lucky to have her as our lead singer."

"No question about it, she's a million times less of a diva than Callista," Bradbury whispered, pressing his face into the cluster of SPACEPOP girls. The band greeted him, not at all surprised to see their biggest fan at the show. Bradbury smirked and added, "A *very* reliable source told me Callista has fired her guitar player four times. She thinks her bandmates are totally interchangeable and can be easily replaced."

"That's not very nice," Hera said.

Bradbury shrugged. "Showbiz." The stage door behind them flew open, and cold, smelly Tik-tik air blew in along with a group of production assistants who were loaded down with microphones and extra stools for the final group performance. Bradbury squeezed his nose closed and exhaled through his mouth. "No wonder Geela didn't show up in person for today's show. It seriously stinks here!"

"Was she *supposed* to be here?" Athena asked, glancing quickly at the other girls. They all moved aside to let the production assistants through with their gear. "Any idea why she isn't?"

"Well," Bradbury said, whispering. "Technically, she *is* here—don't tell anyone she's not. But in fact, she's performing her song for tonight's broadcast in a soundstage on Pluton. They're projecting her hologram into the group so it will look like she's here in person. The producers promised no one would be able to figure out that she isn't actually live with the other girls."

"Why didn't she just come and perform with everyone else?" Hera asked. "She has her own ship—and it's insanely fast. She can get to any planet in the galaxy in less than a few hours."

"Geela hasn't set foot on Tik-tik in weeks," Bradbury said. "This used to be one of her favorite planets, but something happened when her space tankers started flying in and out more often—their fumes mixed with a chemical in the Tik-tik atmosphere and made the whole planet smell like waste."

"How do you know all this?" Juno muttered.

"I keep my ears open," Bradbury said. "Journalist habit."

"So Geela really hasn't been on Tik-tik in weeks?" Rhea asked. Onstage, the director announced that the commercial break was ending and the singers would be on live in thirty seconds—it was time for the final sing-off and Geela's guest appearance. Backstage, the four members of SPACEPOP shared a knowing look—if Geela hadn't set foot on this planet recently, there was no way she could be hiding her most important prisoners here. She herself had said that she enjoyed visiting them in person as often as she could.

"Nope," Bradbury said. "She's been all about Pluton lately. Hey!" he said, snapping his fingers. "Did you guys enter the Battle of the Bands on Pluton? I'd love to see SPACEPOP go head-to-head against Arion IV. You would win for sure!"

"Battle of the Bands?" Athena asked.

"The only requirement is that each band needs to perform a previously unheard song. Something new you've been working on. It's going to be epic!" Bradbury said, his voice so loud someone on the production staff shushed him.

Athena nodded and looked to the other girls. "Think we could have our new song ready in time?"

"New song?" Bradbury said, his eyes wide.

"Something special we've been working on for a while. It's getting very close to being ready," said Athena.

"It *is* ready," Hera said. "It's called 'By My Side,' and it's very special to us."

"'By My Side,'" Athena echoed. "That's perfect, Hera."

"The Battle of the Bands is on Pluton, you say?" asked Rhea. "In Sector Seven, right?"

Bradbury nodded and began to speak. But before he could get any words out, there was a high-pitched, eight-octave trilling scream—and a moment later, the glass in every single one of the camera lenses on set shattered.

CHAPTER 13

EVERYONE SCREAMED AS STAGE LIGHTS BURST and popped, sending colored glass shards everywhere. Bradbury's video screen eyeglass lenses crackled like ice and sprinkled out onto the floor backstage. The camera bots whizzed around, trying to figure out what action to follow. Onstage, each of the singers ducked for cover. Rand raced out onto the stage and covered Luna's body with his own, protecting her from whatever unseen danger was lurking nearby.

It was absolute chaos. The studio went black, production came to a standstill, and backup lights were dragged out to the stage. "It's all right!" someone yelled. "Everyone, calm down."

But for the residents of the Pentangle, the scene felt too familiar—it brought back horrible memories of the day Geela took the royal families prisoner and attacked the five planets of the Pentangle. The noise. The tension. The fear. Even those who hadn't witnessed Geela's take-over live had watched the devastation over and over for days on news feeds.

The five princesses couldn't keep themselves from freaking out. Was Geela closing in on them? Was this some sort of attack, a ploy to get the five remaining royals? Had someone discovered SPACEPOP's secret identities and finally come to collect them?

"Someone's amp malfunctioned!" yelled a director. "Too much feedback. The thing went ballistic and shattered all the glass within a thirty-foot radius. Seriously, folks, calm down. No need to act like divas." He chuckled.

Things onstage began to settle. Rand stood up, helping Luna to her feet. The other sopranos shook themselves off, glaring around at the other girls on stage. "An *amp* is to blame? Whose?" demanded Callista. "What happened?"

Luna shrank away, pulling back from the other singers. From offstage, Athena watched her bandmate pick up the tiny Amp It Up and tuck it under her shirt. Then, head held high, Luna pranced offstage and rushed to her dressing room before anyone had time to ask any further questions. The rest of the band chased after her.

"It was me!" Luna said, flopping down on a sofa with a wide-eyed, wild look on her face. "I ruined the show."

"Not you," Athena said, her voice harsh. "It was the Amp It Up. I told you not to use that awful thing! Your voice sounds incredible without extra volume and pitch support."

"I just wanted to stand out from the crowd during the finale," Luna said, closing her eyes. "I didn't think turning the thing up to level four would cause any problems. That's crazy. Who would manufacture a product with such ridiculous side effects? Breaking glass!"

Bradbury squeezed into Luna's dressing room, bringing an end to the girls' conversation. "Are you okay?" he wheezed. Because his video glasses had shattered, he pulled his phone out of his pocket and began to take video with that. He aimed it at Luna and said, "Since tonight's live broadcast went off the air, it's up to you—Luna!— to tell SPACEPOP fans exactly what happened here today."

Juno stepped in front of his camera. "How about Luna tells you all about it while we travel to Pluton in Sector Seven for the Battle of the Bands?"

"Pluton?" Luna said, her face brightening. She looked at the other girls, eager to hear what she'd missed while she was performing. "Battle of the Bands?"

"Pluton's our next stop," Athena said, nodding. "Come on, Bradbury. We'll give you a lift."

"Oh. My. Grock." Bradbury put his hand over his mouth. "I'm actually *in* the SPACEPOP tour bus. This. Is. AWESOME!" Bradbury traipsed around the band's living room, trying to soak it all in. He was so engrossed in looking at everything that he hadn't yet taken out his phone to get footage for his vlog. "Where do you all sleep? Rehearse?"

"Back there," Juno said, pointing to the back of the bus.

"Can I . . ." Bradbury whispered. "See it?"

"That's where I draw the line," Chamberlin said primly. "I insist that the girls keep a few secrets."

"Speaking of secrets," Bradbury said, finally getting his phone out. He looked serious. "I still wanted to talk to you all about my big reveal. I don't want to ruin anything for the band, obviously, but I do have a pretty important piece of information I've been sitting on. I'm not sure how much longer I can keep your secret a *secret*."

The girls all straightened up, waiting. What did he know?

Bradbury went on, "As a journalist, it's my job to seek the truth and share it with the world."

Chamberlin nervously cleared his throat.

"I've been backstage with you before a few shows now, and I've noticed something . . . about your image," Bradbury said, winking at Luna. "Something the galaxy needs to know about the *real* you."

"How did you find out?" Luna whispered.

Bradbury tapped the edge of his lens-less glasses. "Journalistic observation. You haven't been very good at hiding the truth."

The girls tensed, waiting for him to say what he knew: that they were the princesses of the Pentangle, and he was going to tell the whole galaxy about their cover. This was it—they were ruined. After weeks of searching for the Dungeon of Dark Doom, they had only one last planet to explore. But it was too late. All would be revealed, and Geela would come for them. In no time, they would be joining their parents in the dungeon, and Geela's galactic takeover would be complete.

Bradbury took a deep breath, turned on his camera, and looked right at Luna when he said, "You don't actually use Solar Glow."

Luna blinked at the camera. "What?"

"You can't hide it from me," Bradbury said, nodding. "It's time to come clean."

Juno grabbed the camera out of his hand and switched it off. "*That's* your big secret?" she said.

Bradbury grinned. "It's a doozy, isn't it?"

There was a collective sigh of relief from the girls and Chamberlin. "Bradbury, you found me out," Luna admitted, choking back a giggle. "I don't use Solar Glow."

"So you lied?!" Bradbury said, his voice a whisper. He squeaked, "I *believed* you, Luna. I bought a whole case of Solar Glow products because you told me to!"

Rhea was the first to laugh out loud. But the others joined her a moment later. Soon, even Chamberlin was chuckling. Rand peeked into the room and began to laugh, even though he didn't know what anyone was laughing about—then he charged into the kitchen for a snack. The princesses' pets bounced out of the girls' bedroom, giggling and chittering joyfully.

"What is so funny?" Bradbury demanded, blinking quickly.

"Do you believe *everything* you hear on TV?" Rhea asked. "Or just Luna's product endorsement?" Bradbury shrugged. Rhea arched an eyebrow at Luna and said, "Seems someone *does* believe commercials. Feel a little bad now, Luna?"

Luna groaned. "I obviously need to quit. I can't use my hair to sell something I don't believe in. Their products literally destroy hair—and here I am, convincing people to buy it?" She dropped her head into her hands and groaned again. "Chamberlin, please call the Solar Glow people later and tell them I'm out."

"Bradbury, you know *most* of what's on holo-viz is fake, right?" asked Hera, who had learned the hard way not to fall for strange things people had told her over the years. It seemed she wasn't the only naturally naive one in the room.

"Holo-viz broadcasts don't lie!" Bradbury said. He huffed and said, "I suppose next you're going to try to tell me Geela doesn't use Swish-M-Boots?"

Hera patted him on the shoulder. "Sorry, but no."

Bradbury gasped.

"Also, *The Empress* is totally fake," Luna told him. "You think Geela really will find true love in front of billions of galactic residents?"

"But—" Bradbury spluttered. "But she seemed so happy with her final two choices! I imagine them strolling into the sunset together." He hung his head, crushed.

"*Fight or Flight*?" Juno said. "Is completely rigged. They know who the winner will be even before they begin filming each episode."

"What!" Bradbury gasped. "No!"

Rhea nodded. "And the producers told me who I had to vote for on *Galactic Fashion*."

"They didn't!"

"It's true," Rhea said. "But you can't tell anyone. This has to be our little secret. All of it."

"My lips are sealed!" Bradbury promised. "Thank you for trusting me."

"Can we trust you with one more thing?" Athena asked.

Bradbury nodded vigorously. "Of course! Anything."

Athena asked, "If we play our newest song for you— the one we would debut at the Battle of the Bands—will you let us know what you think?"

"Me?!" Bradbury burst into tears. "Helping SPACEPOP perfect a new song would be my life's greatest honor."

When the space bus landed on Pluton in Sector Seven, it was long past midnight. As soon as Chamberlin blasted away from Tik-Tik, the girls had pulled their instruments into the living room and played their big new song for Bradbury. After their first run-through of "By My Side," he gave them some really helpful suggestions and even pointed out a few places where it would make sense for their pets to jump in with beatboxing. They went through it again, and again, and again.

"I think it's ready," Hera said after their twentieth run-through.

Athena, always a perfectionist, cocked her head and drew in a deep breath. "I never thought I'd say this, but I actually think you might be right—it's finished. We're ready."

"This is going to be the song that really makes you," Bradbury said. "I just know it. And I feel like I'm part of history, since I got to see it come together."

"See it?" Juno said, nudging him. "You helped. You didn't just watch—you were a part of the action, Bradbury. We couldn't have done this without you. Any of what we've done, actually."

Bradbury blushed so deeply that he actually radiated heat from his face. "Thanks," he whispered.

Chamberlin made a bed for Bradbury on the couch, then the girls headed to their room for a little sleep. Because she'd lost their bet, Rhea turned down Luna's sheets for her before she climbed in—then she snuggled into her own bed and fell instantly asleep. But all five girls were woken up only a few hours later when Chamberlin tapped on their door and told them Captain Hansome had sent a messenger droid for them.

The girls crept through the living room, hoping not to

wake Bradbury. The alien stirred as they passed, quietly muttering, "Save me, Juno . . ." in his sleep.

Juno spun around, a look of horror on her face. Meanwhile, the other girls struggled to keep themselves from laughing aloud. Tiptoeing, they continued past Bradbury and his dreams to the ship's control room. As soon as each member of the band had pressed one hand on the droid to unlock the message from the captain, Hansome's voice rang out: "SPACEPOP! Congratulations on securing clearance to land on Pluton. The Resistance wishes you all continued luck during your search for the Dungeon of Dark Doom."

"Thanks, Captain Hansome," Luna said sweetly to the tiny hologram.

The captain's recorded message continued, "We wanted to be sure you are aware that . . . *the Resistance* . . . has received intelligence alerting us that additional security measures have been put into place on Pluton. The capital city has been walled off, and all residents are completely locked out of the city's business district. The city center is, at present, inaccessible. The so-called empress's team has built an impenetrable boundary around the capital."

Chamberlin sunk down in a chair, draping one hand across his forehead. He was already exhausted, just thinking of the mission to come.

Captain Hansome flexed his muscles, grinning. "Our

sources have told . . . *the Resistance* . . . that Geela has suffered a great loss recently. As a result, she has beefed up her security efforts. So this mission will not be easy. Pluton security will be difficult to breach. But . . ." Here, Captain Hansome swallowed and took a deep breath. In a blustery voice he said, "But SPACEPOP, I believe in you. The Resistance has faith that you will find the Dungeon of Dark Doom on Pluton and rescue the royal prisoners."

The tiny hologram fizzled, then disappeared.

"A great loss, eh?" said Rhea. "Think she's sad about her wigs . . . or the little jeweled box?"

"Could be either—or both," said Juno. Luna chewed nervously at her lip.

Hera twisted a curl behind her ear and muttered, "I wish we had stolen that little kwub-kwub cub instead of all those ugly wigs. At least that would have done some good in the universe."

Rhea giggled. "It won't change lives, but we *could* have some fun with the wigs," she said slowly. "What if we ask Rand to hand them out to the audience at the Battle of the Bands? *Someone* should get a little use out of them. And it would totally rock if a bunch of people in the crowd were wearing Geela's hair!"

"I love that idea," Juno said. "I just want them off this bus. If Skitter crawls into my bed wearing one of Geela's wigs one more time, I'm gonna lose it. It's terrifying."

"Oh my Grock, Roxie has been doing the same thing!" Hera said.

"Springle, too," Rhea said. "I hope our pets won't be too sad if we take away their creepy little dress-up wigs."

"We have a plan for the wigs," Luna said. "Are we ready for the rest?"

"We're close," Athena said after a long moment. "Knowing there are such extreme security measures in place on Pluton makes me think we're on the right track." She took a deep breath and smiled one of her rare smiles. "I think today is the day we will find our families and take back the galaxy."

CHAPTER 14

SPACEPOP ARRIVED ON THE PLANET PLUTON FOR THE BATTLE OF THE BANDS . . .

WHO NEEDS A NEW HAIRDO?

YOU WANT A WIG?

173

WHERE SHOULD I SET UP ALL OUR STUFF?

FOLLOW ME. SPACEPOP, WE'LL MEET YOU AT THE STAGE!

I THOUGHT HANSOME WAS EXAGGERATING . . . BUT THERE IS AN **ACTUAL** WALL KEEPING EVERYONE OUT OF THE CITY CENTER!

HOW ARE WE SUPPOSED TO GET TO THE OTHER SIDE?

MAYBE **YOU** COULD BOUNCE OVER, SPRINGLE . . . BUT WE AREN'T SENDING YOU IN THERE ALONE!

CALM DOWN, ROXIE. YOU CAN'T FIGHT A WALL.

WHILE WAITING FOR THEIR TURN TO PERFORM, THE REBELS TRIED EVERYTHING THEY COULD THINK OF TO GET PAST GEELA'S LOCKED WALL.

THE WALL WAS TOO STRONG FOR SKITTER TO BREAK THROUGH.

ADORA COULDN'T CHARM THE GUARDS INTO UNLOCKING THE GATES.

THE WALL WAS SO HIGH, EVEN SPRINGLE COULDN'T BOUNCE OVER.

WHEEEEE!

AND FIERCE LITTLE ROXIE COULDN'T BASH IT OPEN.

CAPOW!

GRUNT!

WE'RE GOING TO HAVE TO FIGURE THIS OUT AFTER THE SHOW.

IT WAS ALMOST SPACEPOP'S TURN TO BATTLE. BUT FIRST, ARION IV STEPPED INTO THE SPOTLIGHT!

THIS BATTLE OF THE BANDS HAS SOME TOUGH COMPETITION.

NOTHING WE CAN'T HANDLE.

YOUR NEW SONG IS **SO** MUCH BETTER THAN ANYTHING I'VE HEARD TONIGHT!

179

THE REBELS HID IN THE CROWD TO SLIP PAST THE GUARDS AND INTO THE CITY CENTER UNDETECTED.

THAT WAS AN AMAZING IDEA TO BREAK THROUGH THE WALL, ATHENA!

THIS TIME I **WANTED** THE AMP IT UP TO MALFUNCTION!

DO YOU THINK WE WON THE BATTLE OF THE BANDS?

DOES IT REALLY MATTER?

THE GIRLS FOUND GEELA'S BUILDING AND FOUGHT THEIR WAY INSIDE.

CHEEP CHEEP!!

183

GO, ROXIE. RESCUE THE KWUB-KWUB!

COME ON, HERA. WE NEED TO KEEP MOVING!

YOU'RE SAFE NOW.

UH-OH!

IT'S FINALLY THE RIGHT TIME TO TRY THE HYPNO-GLASSES!

BZZZZT!

IS THIS IT?!

WE CAN'T FIGHT THEM ALL. WE HAVE TO WAIT UNTIL THEY'RE GONE TO GET THE DOOR OPEN.

SOLAR GLOW

SWISH-M BOOTS

SWISH-M BOOTS

I THINK IT IS TIME FOR A CHANGE OF SCENERY. PLUTON IS NO LONGER SECURE. WE MUST MOVE THE PRISONERS.

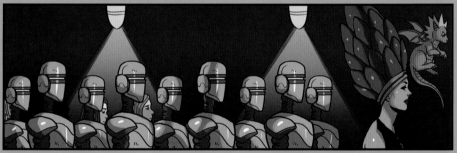

LET'S GO!

CHAPTER 15

THE AIR WAS STILL AND QUIET INSIDE THE deserted hangar. None of the SPACEPOP rebels said anything for a long time. They watched, devastated, as the ship carrying their parents—and their only remaining hope of overthrowing Geela—blasted out of Pluton's atmosphere.

After a long silence, Athena whispered, "We lost them again."

Juno swiped at her face to try to erase the tears that wouldn't stop falling. "We should have fought," she growled. "We could have saved them. We just let them go; we *let* Geela take them again!"

"There are only five of us," Rhea said. From down on

the floor, Springle meeped. She and the other space pets gathered around the girls to join the group. Rhea nodded and said, "Okay, yeah—so there were ten of us. But it would have been ten of us going up against dozens of guards *and* Geela. Your parents were right—it does no one any good if we are caught, too."

Hera sniffled. "We came so close." From inside her suit, the kwub-kwub purred. It nuzzled against Hera's chest, providing a brief moment of comfort.

"Obviously, this is a setback," Athena said, turning to lead the group out of the hangar. It was time to go. They had to get back to the ship and give Hansome and Chamberlin an update. "And a major disappointment. Today was not our victory. But I, for one, have renewed hope."

"You watched Geela blast into space with our parents *again*, and you have renewed hope?" Juno snapped, dragging her feet as she tromped after the group.

"We know they're all okay," Athena explained. "We've seen them with our own eyes now, so we know that they're still alive and well. And even better, *they* now know someone is trying to find them. We have given *them* hope! I dearly wish that knowledge will help keep our families' spirits up through the next chapter of their journey. And if we don't want them to lose hope—we must not, either."

"That sounds like a lot of ridiculous, Hera-style optimism," Rhea grumbled bitterly. "You're usually more practical than that. Come on, Athena. We lost. Geela won. Can we all just face the facts?"

"No, no. Athena's right," Hera said quickly. "The *worst* thing we could do now is give up." She rubbed the kwub-kwub's head—the smell of its soft fur calmed her. "We got a second chance to save the kwub-kwub and get it away from Geela, didn't we? The same thing could—*will!*—happen with our parents."

Athena nodded. "We didn't win the war today . . . but we haven't lost yet, either. We can either see this as an opportunity for renewed focus on the mission, or we accept it as our stopping point."

Luna linked her arm through Hera's. "We found them once; we'll find them again. There is absolutely no reason we can't track Geela to her next hiding spot. And next time, we won't let them slip away. Maybe today isn't the day we conquer Geela, but that day *will* come."

Juno and Rhea exchanged wary glances. "Okay," Rhea said finally, sighing. "You're right. No giving up now."

"We carry on," said Juno.

"We carry on," repeated Athena.

☆ ☆ ☆ ☆ ☆

When the girls and their pets finally got back to the space bus, Bradbury was pacing back and forth in front of the door, looking extremely agitated. "Where have you been?" he demanded. He gaped at the band and blurted out, "And what are you wearing?"

Rhea glanced down at her black rebel suit and thought fast. "These are our, uh, relaxing outfits," she said, shrugging. "Like a robe. But jet-black and fitted and stretchy."

"Oh," Bradbury said, calming a bit. "They look nice."

"Thanks," Juno said. Rhea's quick comebacks definitely served a useful purpose from time to time. Calling their rebel suits *robes* was a stretch, but Bradbury seemed to buy the lie. "Bradbury, these relaxing suits are yet another thing we should probably keep secret, okay? Don't tell anyone about what we wear behind the curtain—deal? It just doesn't fit our image."

"Of course, of course! Anything for you, Juno," Bradbury promised. He threw out his arms and asked again, "But where have you been? The party in Pluton has been over for half an hour! I was worried when I couldn't find you anywhere! I lost you when the wall shattered, and then there were crowds everywhere, and—"

"Sorry, Bradbury." Luna cut him off. The girls' pets hopped past and scurried into the bus. After the day's adventure, they were all eager to curl up for a much-needed nap. Luna watched them go, dreaming of the moment she would lay her own head on her pillow. "It's—well, it's kind of complicated."

Bradbury pouted. "I get it."

"It really is complicated," Athena assured him. "I'm sorry, Bradbury. It's been a long couple of nights. We're all pretty eager to get out of here."

"Yeah, I said I get it," Bradbury said sadly. He hung his head. "I'll just leave now. I met up with some friends after the Battle of the Bands. They can give me a ride back to Pallomo."

"Hey," Hera said, suddenly thinking of an idea of how to cheer him up. "I almost forgot—I have something for you."

"For me?" Bradbury said, brightening.

"A special present," Hera said, nodding happily. She pulled the kwub-kwub cub out of her rebel suit and dropped the little critter into Bradbury's arms. "This little critter is very special to me—he's one of my friends from the adoption event. It's my duty to find the perfect home for him, and I think you can provide that."

"A kwub-kwub!" Bradbury said, nuzzling the little pet. "Just like Geela has?!"

"Um," Hera said, cringing. "Yeah, in a way it's a little like Geela's. But this kwub-kwub can be yours—if you're willing to care for him and promise to bring him over to visit me every once in a while? I want you to be sure you can take care of him before I leave him with you."

"I've always wanted a kwub-kwub!" Bradbury said, gushing. "I love him! Thank you!" He gazed lovingly at the kwub-kwub and then turned his starry eyes toward Hera.

"Uh-oh," Luna muttered to Juno. "Looks like Bradbury might have a new crush now . . ."

"I'll survive," Juno whispered back.

"Can I take a picture of the two of you together?" Hera asked. "You look so cute!" She raced inside the space bus, returning a moment later with her camera. Bradbury snuggled his face into the kwub-kwub's fur and smiled at the camera. As Hera snapped the picture, she hoped Geela had spent little enough time with the tiny pet that if she ever saw pictures of him anywhere online, she wouldn't even recognize the fuzzball. It was worth the risk—the kwub-kwub would have a wonderful life with Bradbury, and Bradbury clearly had room in his life for someone to love.

"Thanks, Hera," Bradbury said again. "This is the best gift ever."

"Hearing you say that . . ." Hera said, tearing up, "is a gift to me." She wrapped her arms around Bradbury and the kwub-kwub cub.

Rhea groaned—loudly—and rolled her eyes.

"Bradbury, thanks again for everything these past few days," Athena said. "We appreciate everything you do for us so very much. I hope you know that." Bradbury nodded quickly. "We'll see you soon?"

"Very soon!" Bradbury said. "Thanks for the lift to Pluton. I hope you have a great trip to wherever you're going next." He began to walk away, then turned back. "Oh, and did you know you won the Battle of the Bands?"

"We did?" Rhea asked.

Bradbury grinned. "I heard someone say it was a unanimous decision. The judges all loved you and especially loved the *end* of your show—it was very exciting. And of course, I agree with the judges." He held up the kwub-kwub and said in a silly voice, "So do I!" They all laughed. Then Bradbury switched back to his normal voice and asked, "So where is SPACEPOP off to next?"

The girls all glanced at one another. After a few seconds, Rhea shrugged. "Not sure yet," she said. "Time to make a plan."

Bradbury winked behind his lens-less glasses. "I'll find you."

When they got into the ship, Captain Hansome was already waiting for them on the Resistance's secure holo-network. "Geela is on the move," he announced.

"Yes," Athena said. "We know." The girls told the captain and Chamberlin every detail of their mission on Pluton. They told them about the wall, how they had used the Amp It Up, their successful infiltration into Geela's headquarters, their brief conversation with the prisoners. "And then she led them into a ship and took them away—again."

Hansome took a deep breath and scratched his stubbly chin. "I see."

"We're so, so sorry," Luna sobbed. "They were right there, within our reach, and we let them go."

"You had no other choice." Hansome confirmed what the girls had already figured out for themselves. "You made the right decision. Geela has made it very clear that any rebel who is caught will be destroyed. Had you tried to fight, we would have lost you *and* the prisoners."

"We're not going to stop searching until they are safe," Juno promised. "You have our word."

Chamberlin let out a small groan when he realized what this meant.

Hansome nodded seriously. "All of us here at *the Resistance* appreciate your dedication very much. We will be in touch to discuss the next steps. Stay strong, and get some rest."

"Captain Hansome?" Luna said, stepping forward so she was right in Hansome's line of sight. "Before you go, we found something on Lud that we think may have been Geela's. We didn't have a chance to show you before now, but perhaps it could be of some use?" She held up the small, jewel-encrusted box they had found in Geela's treasure room on Lud, keeping it still in the palm of her hand so Hansome could see it clearly through the holo-gram. "Do you know what this might be and if it has any meaning?"

Hansome's face registered shock, and then he pumped his fist in the air. Smiling broadly, the captain announced, "This, SPACEPOP? This changes *everything*."

ABOUT THE AUTHOR

ERIN DOWNING has written more than fifty books for young adults, tweens, and kids, including *SPACEPOP: Not Your Average Princesses*, *Best Friends (Until Someone Better Comes Along)*, *A Funny Thing About Love*, and *Moon Shadow* (in stores summer 2017). She also writes both The Quirks and Puppy Pirates series (as Erin Soderberg). Before becoming an author, Erin was a book editor and a cookie inventor, and she also worked for Nickelodeon. When she's not writing, Erin plays guitar, reads, watches TV, and—like Luna—dreams of a life with a butler, maid service, and a personal chef. She lives in Minneapolis, Minnesota, with her husband, kids, and a very fluffy dog. More information about Erin's books can be found at erindowning.com.